THE
BATTLE ROYALE
BR
SLAM BOOK

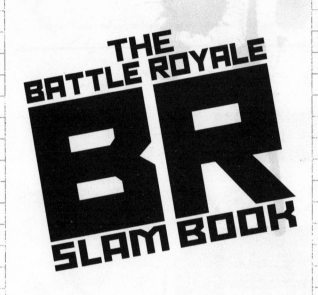

HAIKA
SORU

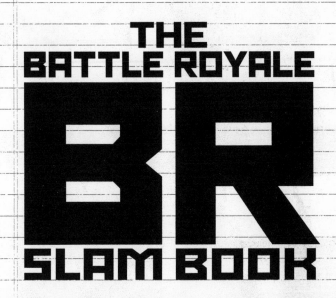

THE BATTLE ROYALE
BR
SLAM BOOK

ESSAYS ON THE CULT CLASSIC BY KOUSHUN TAKAMI

Edited by NICK MAMATAS
and MASUMI WASHINGTON

HAIKA SORU

SAN FRANCISCO

THE BATTLE ROYALE SLAM BOOK
© 2014 VIZ Media
Copyright for individual essays remain the property of their authors.

Cover art by Tomer Hanuka
Design by Fawn Lau

HAIKASORU
Published by VIZ Media, LLC
PO Box 77010
San Francisco, CA 94107

www.haikasoru.com

Library of Congress Cataloging-in-Publication Data
Battle Royale slam book : essays on the cult classic by Koushun Takami /
edited by Nick Mamatas and Masumi Washington.
     pages cm
   ISBN 978-1-4215-6599-6 (pbk.)
 1. Takami, Koushun. Batoru rowaiaru. I. Mamatas, Nick, editor of
compilation. II. Washington, Masumi, editor of compilation.
  PL876.A393B39 2014
  895.63'6—dc23
                           2014001629

Printed in the U.S.A.
First printing, April 2014

CONTENTS

Blood in the Classroom, Blood on the Page: Will *Battle Royale* Ever Be on the Test?

It's one of the secrets of literary immortality—one generation's cult novel becomes the next generation's assigned reading. Most high schoolers today find J.D. Salinger's *Catcher in the Rye* to be a total bore. The kid's a whiner, and there isn't even all that much sex or cursing in the book, despite all the warnings-cum-promises of nervous school board members. The controversies of the 1950s aren't even parental memories. Maybe Grandma remembers what all the fuss was about. But back in the day, *Catcher in the Rye* was an occult text, a sign of membership in a secret club of the Misunderstood Who Understand.

And it's hardly the only novel that was once so meaningful to awkward young literary men and women who grew up to be high school English teachers: *The Great Gatsby* by F. Scott Fitzgerald took decades to win its place in American letters and in the standard curriculum. That the 1925 novel was an issued text to soldiers fighting in the Second World War helped. One wouldn't think a story of fancy parties and whispered secrets would mean much to fighting men, but it did. Indeed, *Gatsby* entered WWII, and *Catcher* came out of WWII. Salinger was typing up Holden Caulfield stories while his position was being shelled by the Nazis. William Golding's dystopian *Lord of the Flies*—the book to which *Battle Royale* is most frequently, and inaccurately, compared—also came directly out of the horrors of that war.

Today, the anger, alienation, and anxieties that fueled these books have been reduced to test questions and essay prompts. At Boston Latin, one of the country's premier schools, kids are told to aspire toward a "green light," just like Gatsby did in the novel. The kids dutifully write that their green lights are earning a black belt or getting into medical school. An almost exact inversion of Fitzgerald's view of that light across the harbor as "the orgastic future that year by year recedes before us."

And the same happens to the other former cult novels, from *Catcher* to *The Chocolate War.* They are defanged, domesticated. *The Lord of the Flies,* whose theme is the tension between democratic civilization and the will to power, becomes a lesson on the importance of following the rules in school and the workplace, to name two very undemocratic social structures. *Catcher,* its social cachet long since exhausted, has devolved into an exercise in which students get good grades by writing phony essays about a kid who hates phonies and drops out of school.

If there's a cult novel for today's youth, it's Koushun Takami's *Battle Royale.* It is, in many ways, the opposite of *Lord of the Flies,* and rather more like the former cult novel that became the assigned reading for my late-1980s generation, Robert Cormier's 1974 *The Chocolate War.* Society isn't what keeps us from devolving into savagery, it *is* the savagery. You know the basics of *Battle Royale*'s story by now: in a future dystopia, junior high school children are kidnapped by the government, outfitted with explosive collars and an array of weapons, and forced to kill one another. The beauty of the novel is that most children try to resist in one way or another. Suicides, forming groups and trying to leave the action, working on escape plans, or just running and hiding; these are all better ideas than actually playing the game. The few students who do engage in the game are either simply terrified or embrace the game with enthusiasm thanks to mental illness or histories of horrifying abuse.

And a few of the kids actually win. Win for real. The tamper-proof collars are disabled, the inescapable island fled from, the diabolical teacher slain. And they're left with nothing but one another in a world arrayed against them. As a moral lesson, it's one far superior to most of the former cult novels turned classics we're made to read in school.

Cult novels find their audience because they are about something. (Most novels are sadly about nothing, whereas the true classics are about many things and thus invite multiple competing readings.) And that something—usually some social criticism—is easy enough for kids to understand. And those few kids of every generation who find their book and read it till the pages fall from the spine, who buy tens of copies of it and press it on their friends and acquaintances, they mostly grow up to know that the rat race of big business and monetary success is empty and shallow. But nobody gets paid just to read interesting books, so our sensitive cultists end up teaching high school and find themselves faced with the same bullies and creeps who terrorized them in their own school days. *But if only these kids would just read my favorite book, maybe they'd understand . . .*

But no, most people never understand. "Bullshit" is a verb, as in "I didn't do the reading; I'll have to bullshit my way through this essay about *The Chocolate War*." They don't understand and don't want to understand. They want their easy A, their diploma, and then their black belt and well-paying job as a doctor. You don't need to know that the conch in *Lord of the Flies* represents social democracy to set someone's broken toe or to invest heavily in palladium futures.

The Battle Royale Slam Book is for people who understand, by people who understand. There is an alternative to schoolteaching, albeit a risky one, for bookish teens. They can become writers. The writers in this volume are successful, or not; best sellers, or obscure; university scholars, or blue-collar high school grads. Their essays are meaningful, personal, enthusiastic. There are no easy As in this anthology, no bullshit. We're telling you how it is, even when we disagree with one another. The cult of *Battle Royale* remains strong, fifteen years after the novel's first publication in Japan and ten after its English translation was published. Welcome to school. Read the slam book, write your own notes on the blank pages at the end, then pass it along.

But fifteen years is only half a generation. Hey you! Dear Reader! Will you get your degree and head back to high school to teach the kids what the world's all about through the magic of books? By the time the thirtieth anniversary of *Battle Royale* rolls around, will the book be neutered, defanged, and ready for mass consumption by sullen high schoolers? Maybe not. Unlike *Gatsby, Catcher,* et al., *Battle Royale* is long. A veritable epic of slaughter. It's hard enough to get kids to read short books. Nobody is going to bank on getting the little twerps to read a six-hundred-page novel for school. (For fun, yes. Hundreds of thousands of you have joined the cult already!) Of course, there's a film version, which until recently was difficult to legally screen in the United States. And it's even gorier than the book. For now, we are safe. No substitute teacher who wants to keep his or her job is going to break out the *Battle Royale* DVD on a rainy Thursday afternoon.

Most importantly, *Battle Royale* is ultimately about something that resists domestication. You can't turn it into a tale of ambition and success, like *Gatsby*, nor a work extolling the virtues of law and order like *Lord of the Flies. BR*'s sheer body count hammers home the lesson that *The Chocolate War* only alludes to—the world is a horrible place, and authority can never be trusted. And *Catcher?* The problem is that, yes, the world is full of phonies, but what are you going to do about it? According to Salinger, sulk. According to Koushun Takami, you *fight*. Fight in every way, against all possible expressions of authority; no bureaucrat could ever sanitize that theme sufficiently for essay prompts and multiple choice questions. One can see it now:

1. In a battle royale, the best thing to do is:
   A. Hide and cower and wait to be picked off.
   B. Kill yourself.
   C. Play to win! Kill as many people as possible!
   D. Work with your friends to overthrow the game and

escape from society, starting with the person who handed you this test.

And honestly, if any circa 2013 high schooler who likes to read ends up an English teacher ten years from now, he or she will probably just make the students read *The Hunger Games* instead. It's short, and the movie is rated PG-13.

The correct answer is D. Be untamable, fight against the battle royale. Let this book be your guide.

—Nick Mamatas
New Year's Eve, 2013

Death for Kids

BY JOHN SKIPP

Oh, kids. They grow up so fast. Unless somebody kills them. Or they kill each other.

It's only natural to want to protect them, of course. And not just their lives, but their innocence. That said, life is what happens when we're making other plans. And death shows up whenever, and for whomever, the fuck it wants.

Speaking personally: I saw my first dying people within half an hour of landing at Ministro Pistarini International Airport, just outside Buenos Aires. It was 1966, and I was eight years old.

We'd just taken a Boeing 707—the largest craft in the fleet of Aerolineas Argentinas—from Washington, D.C., care of the US State Department. My dad's mysterious new government job had brought the family from Milwaukee to Arlington, VA, for six months of prep, before launching us deep into the other America.

I have jumbled memories of landing and negotiating customs, lugging our baggage as we followed the guy with the driver's cap and the sign marked SKIPP to the sleek sedan taking us to our new home. All I can say for sure is that I had the window seat in the back, on the driver's side—and that we were less than ten minutes down the Richerri Motorway—when I saw the cloud of dirt and rock from the edge of the overpass ahead.

There was a bus, hurtling sideways and over the brink, like a train derailed. I couldn't see the shattering glass, but I could see the screaming faces. Blood on some, poking through the broken windows. Others pressed against the glass as yet remaining.

Then we were under the overpass, me whipping backward in my seat to watch the bus plummet downward, then disappear from view. Our driver did not slow for a second.

That was my first genuine childhood glimpse.

Once we settled in the suburb of San Isidro, in a very nice two-story house with a swimming pool and bars on the windows, I began to explore. Making friends with the local kids and learning Spanish a trillion times faster than the rest of my family combined. The neighborhood boys kicked my ass at *futbol* until I got the gist of the game and earned their respect. At which point, they started showing me the ropes.

It was a fifteen-block walk from my house to the San Isidro station. From there, I took the commuter train three stops to La Lucila, where El Colegio Lincoln was, the school for US government, military, or corporate kids, as well as wealthy Anglo-Argentinos.

About three blocks along the way, there was a car full of dried blood and bullet holes, pulled up at the curb right next to a local bodega. I was informed that it had belonged to a couple of local fuck-ups who thought that robbing a bank might be a good idea.

At that time in Buenos Aires, even traffic cops carried submachine guns—one of the perks of a police state. And they had totally Bonnie and Clyde-ed that car, swiss-cheesing it with hundreds of rounds that I spent countless hours, in youthful awe, cataloging.

So if that bullet went through the door here, I noted, peering through the metal hole, *that explains that gouge in the driver's seat and this splash of blood on the rear upholstery. Whereas these seven holes sawed right across the side, on either side. So which was the entry, and which was the exit?* A forensic pathologist at the age of eight.

That car was left sitting at the curb for nearly a year, as a constant reminder that if you messed with them—if you robbed a bank—they would kill the living shit out of you. The urban equivalent of a head on a medieval pike.

But it didn't fully occur to me that little kids could die like that until I watched two ten-year-olds beat a six-year-old to death on the San Isidro train platform, from the other side of the tracks.

The six-year-old was a beautiful boy. Very popular with the Americans, whose shoes he shined as they waited for the train. He could barely lug his wooden shoeshine box, tiny as he was. But people loved him for that: an adorable novelty with a keepsake smile. Like a luminous virgin on shoeshine prostitution row.

One morning, it just became too much for the competition. They beat his brains in, then out of his skull, with his own shoeshine box. Then ran off. I never saw them again.

But I saw what happened.

Not too long after that, I found *Lord of the Flies* in the school library. And it, more than anything, helped me process what I was seeing all around me. I kept coming back to the death of Simon, his body floating in the water. And poor Piggy, as both his skull and the conch that signified civilization were shattered.

This, I realized, was what happened when we lost our way.

Over the next four years, I bore witness to a lot more blood and death. Saw futbol stadium staircases stream with the blood of trampled hundreds on my tenth birthday. Saw Chilean immigrants beaten by armed police right outside my school fence, during lunchtime recess. Ultimately fled the country, running down the street with screaming thousands as armored tanks rolled down the central boulevard, en route to overthrowing Presidente Ongania. Barely got out of the country in time to miss the Generalisimo of the Month Club, and the Black Hand, and the thousands more who wound up disappeared, their mass graves only discovered decades later.

In short, I saw far more horror at an early age than any young man should.

But I learned a hell of a lot. A healthy disrespect for authority, just for starters. A fierce opposition to injustice. An even fiercer love for the underdog. And a keen sense of allegiance with those who did not forget themselves, and forfeit their souls, when shit got hard. Because shit would always be hard.

It's a beautiful, ugly world.

Which brings us back to *Battle Royale*.

I remember full well the controversy that surrounded this film upon its release. Was lucky enough to get a bootleg VHS of it, well before it officially hit America. Knew that I was supposed to be morally appalled by the spectacle of kids killing kids. Of kids dying at all.

But honestly? I just felt ratified and tremendously proud of everyone involved from the author of the book to the makers of the film, including every single member of the cast and crew.

To me, the greatness of *Battle Royale* lies not just in its cinematic savagery, but in its deep and wide-ranging emotional acuity. The perfectly captured teenage sweetness of friendship, and crushes, and love, juxtaposed against crushing totalitarian madness and the horrible harvest it reaps.

It's a truly great film because it doesn't hold back on *anything*. It doesn't pick one note, sweet or sour, and hammer it monochromatically into the ground, like so many of the legendary transgressive films it often winds up on all those "100 Most Fucked-Up" lists with.

It goes symphonic, orchestrally layering its high and low registers in radical juxtaposition. So that you're laughing one minute, crying the next, flinching and going "Holy *shit*!" before you have a chance to look away.

It is, in short, profound. And therefore profoundly moving.

No matter what age you are, when it hits.

When I showed it to my early-teenage daughters, then ages fifteen and thirteen, they were thoroughly blown away. As I knew they would be. We watched it together, hugging as needed. Hitting pause once or twice, just to process and discuss what we'd just seen. But mostly plowing through.

And then—at their request—watching it again.

Next thing I knew, they were showing it to their slumber party friends, whose parents would no doubt have thought it unthinkable to subject their tender lumplings to such frank, unflinching horror.

But again and again, I found these kids (mostly girls) not just jacked up on the craziness, but honestly grateful that someone was telling them these terrible truths. That the nightmares beyond *Goosebumps* and *Are You Afraid of the Dark?* were being laid bare for them, in much the same way as those bullet holes in the bank-robbing car told me the truth about how things really are. Minus having to watch a little boy beaten to death in real life, right in front of them.

It was no surprise to me when—many years later—*The Hunger Games* became a huge hit. It was just a matter of time before some-body sanitized this kind of story for mainstream use. And I frankly applaud it.

I only wish that the majority of nice American kids got to watch *Battle Royale* first. Because it hits harder, and truer. Doesn't pussy out on the meat of the matter. Doesn't couch it in conventionally heroic terms. (Much as I love Katniss, most of us—young or otherwise—would not rise so archetypally to the occasion. We would bumble through, at best. Or otherwise succumb.)

Which is to say:

From cradle to grave, death chases us, not giving two shits whether we think it's age-appropriate. It takes us by surprise, and more often than not finds us woefully unprepared.

I love innocence as much as the next guy. But I'm glad I got a head start on the horror, got to look the world straight in the eye early on. It gave me a lot fewer illusions to burn through and still left me with more than enough to keep me guessing till the end.

Who we are, given the hands we're dealt—who we hope to be, where we take our stand, and how we handle the beautiful, horrible, unjust and unstoppable love and chaos of our lives . . .

That's our Battle Royale.

Choose wisely.

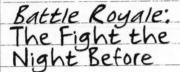

Battle Royale: The Fight the Night Before

BY MASAO HIGASHI

TRANSLATED BY JOCELYNE ALLEN

I was one of the first people in Japan to read Koushun Takami's *Battle Royale*. I remember it being soon after New Year's in 1998, over a year before the book was published by Ohta Publishing in April 1999. The thick, bundled manuscript showed up in a cardboard box sent by Kadokawa Shoten, a major Japanese publisher. An entry in the Fifth Japan Horror Novel Award competition, it arrived at my door because I was a member of the preliminary selection committee.

Allow me to explain briefly here the selection process for this particular prize. The Japan Horror Novel literary prize was set up in 1994 under the joint sponsorship of Kadokawa Shoten and Fuji Television (one of Japan's main TV broadcasters), the first public award in Japan focusing on the horror genre. Prizes are awarded in two categories—novel and short story—and submissions are accepted for works that "depict the light and darkness of humanity through terror."

Although only honorable mentions were given with no prize-winning works in its founding year, the grand prize winner in the second year—the sci-fi horror *Parasite Eve* by Hideaki Sena—went on to become a best seller, unprecedented for a horror novel. Yusuke Kishi's suspense horror *Kuroi Ie* (Black House), winner of the fourth grand prize, has also been an enduring long-seller and received tremendous attention, having been made into a film not only in Japan, but also in Korea.

This same prize has since turned out an impressive number of talented writers one after another, such as Yasumi Kobayashi, Shimako Iwai, Osamu Makino, Kotaro Tsunekawa, Minato Shukawa, Ko Amemura, and Seia Tanabe. It would likely not be any exaggeration to say that it was this prize that allowed the horror genre to become established in the world of Japanese popular literature.

Selection for the prize takes place in three stages. The initial screening is done by a preliminary selection committee made up of about seven literary critics and reviewers versed in horror and about ten in-house editors, who divide up and read all the submissions. The works selected at this stage are then discussed in a preliminary selection meeting of this committee (secondary screening), and the final nominated works that come out of this screening are read by the final selection committee, which is made up of several famous authors. Then, a final selection meeting is held to decide on the winners of the grand prize, novel prize, and short story prize.

The final selection committee for the fifth award was comprised of three authors: Hiroshi Aramata, Katsuhiko Takahashi, and Mariko Hayashi. Aramata, in addition to being known for his occult romance series *Teito Monogatari* (Tales of the Capital), which was also made into a movie, is an expert in fantasy and occult literature and natural history, and has produced numerous critical works and translations in these fields. Takahashi is a Naoki Prize-winning (the most prestigious award in the world of Japanese popular literature) author, working not only in horror, but a broad range of genres from science fiction romance to serious historical novels. Hayashi has also won the Naoki Prize and enjoys broad appeal as a writer of romance novels and essays for women.

Now, to see what these three authors had to say about *Battle Royale* at the fifth selection committee meeting on March 20, 1998, I'll quote from the committee report published in that year's June issue of the magazine *Hon no Tabibito* (The Book Traveler). (Incidentally, this particular year finished with no work selected in either category.)

First, Hiroshi Aramata: "It was quite an uncomfortable thing to have ended up with something like *Battle Royale,* which appears to be a direct parody of *Kinpachi Sensei.* I suppose it was intentional, but in any case, nearly everything, right down to the way the story is told, is a parody of the TV show. Given that, together with the structure of forty-two students killing each other one by one, I felt there might just be too many problems with the work. I was also concerned at how, for some reason, the tension is toned down as you proceed into the second half. I think that in terms of story, structure, and subject matter, this work was the most well done, but I also feared that putting out this *Kinpachi Sensei* as is would bring about a number of problems."

The "Kinpachi Sensei" here refers to the hot-blooded junior high teacher with a heart of gold from the TV show *3-Nen B-Gumi Kinpachi Sensei* (Grade Nine, Class B Teacher Kinpachi), which boasted a high viewership over its many years on the air as a paragon of the Japanese school drama. And it is true that, as Aramata noted, there are aspects of *Battle Royale* that invert to the dark side the peculiarly Japanese school drama as represented by *Kinpachi Sensei.* I cannot deny this aspect likely ended up being one reason the book sparked such a huge reaction in society upon its publication.

Seeing Aramata's disapproval, Katsuhiko Takahashi had the following to say. "At best, my assessment is within the context of these four works, and although I did feel that *Battle Royale* was the superior work in terms of its construction as a novel, I did feel that giving the prize at a time like this to a work that has junior high school students killing each other would be a definite negative for the Horror Prize. In fact, I came today with the idea that in this sense, when I pushed this work, Aramata and Hayashi had perhaps no choice but to take opposing positions."

I believe that the "time like this" Takahashi speaks of refers to the fact that precisely at that time, the country's decaying educational structure was dubbed "classroom chaos" and taken up by the media as a societal problem.

And then we have Mariko Hayashi's comments. "I do believe that *Battle Royale* is the best of the four novels here, but it was like being made to read an unpleasant near-future manga. No matter how squarely it might be horror or how interesting it might be, I'm not so sure we should be writing stories like this."

Put simply, the three authors, while recognizing *Battle Royale*'s value as a novel, fiercely rejected the premise of the book: junior high school students repeatedly and mercilessly killing each other. Seen from our perspective now, fifteen years after the fact, the reactions of these three authors naturally appear somewhat excessive, and opinion is likely divided on whether or not current societal mores should be brought into the world of storytelling, which is from the start a product of the imagination.

Nevertheless, taking into consideration the situation horror lovers in Japan were put in at the time, we start to see that this kind of excessive reaction was essentially unavoidable.

On May 27, 1997, the severed head of a developmentally delayed elementary school boy was discovered at the gates of a junior high school in Suma Ward in Kobe, Hyogo—a scenic location well known as one of the settings of *The Tale of Genji*. This was the curtain rising on what the world would call the Sakakibara Incident. The mouth of the head of the deceased held a note from the killer taking responsibility for the crime. The text of that note was as follows.

So the game begins.
You stupid police
Just try and stop me.
For me, killing is a tremendous pleasure.
I want to watch people die so much I can hardly stand it.
Punishment by death for the filthy vegetables.
Judgment of bloodshed for many years of great bitterness.
            SHOOLL [sic] *KILL*
                        —School killer Sakakibara

The murderer, arrested approximately a month later, on June 28, was an ordinary fourteen-year-old boy attending the junior high school where the head had been found. He was also suspected in a series of child murders that had occurred earlier in the same area. In addition to the bizarre nature of the crime and the unique note at the scene, the fact that the murderer was a junior high school student set off powerful reverberations throughout society. You may even recall that the case was widely reported on in American media including the *Washington Post* and the *New York Times*.

Because horror movies and violent manga were found in the boy's room, inevitably there was a growing wave of so-called "horror bashing" calling for the legal regulation of videos and other media featuring scenes of brutality, all of which served to stigmatize horror lovers.

Then, as the aftereffects of these attacks still lingered, a horror novel appeared depicting a slaughter among battling junior high school students, as if to make real the words from the killer's note "So the game begins" and "I want to watch people die so much I can hardly stand it." Which is why we are forced to conclude that the confusion, indignation, and apprehension of the members of the selection committee were eminently reasonable.

To speak personally, reading *Battle Royale* at the preliminary selection stage, I found the work itself a very fine read. Even compared with the other candidates for the novel prize—Keita Tokaji's *Century of the Damned,* Kei Yanagihara's *Yoru ni nemurenu monotachi e* (To Those Who Can't Sleep at Night), and Masahiko Hoshina's *Kugustu no yorokobi* (The Puppet's Pleasure) (incidentally, these three authors later went on to make their professional debuts)—I felt that it was a superior work. Now to speak of whether or not my verdict was a favorable one, regrettably, I recall that I did not push it all that actively.

The reason was simple. By my own standards, having advocated a supernatural terror fundamentalism (the mainstream position that considers terror through the supernatural to be horror) in the past, I was forced to conclude that the fear *Battle Royale* evokes is of a different nature than that found in horror.

Happiest Days of Your Life: *Battle Royale* and School Fiction

BY ADAM ROBERTS

If you're reading this, you went to school. School is where we learn skills such as reading, writing, and the importance of that initial "a" in the word *arithmetic*. But a school is about more than its curriculum. It's where we make friends; it's what structures our lives for a dozen years—longer, if we go on to college. It is our gateway to the world of adult life. In fact, let's push the boat out shall we? School days are the happiest days of our lives. School is a haven from the stresses and violence of the adult world. An Eden of innocence.

It's easy to forget that *Battle Royale* is a school novel. It does, of course, tell a story about forty-two Japanese schoolchildren, but what happens to those kids is pretty far removed from most kids' school experience. I don't know about you, but my old school was considerably less lethal.

In fact, very little of the text concerns the day-to-day business of schooling. Koushun Takami's novel starts with the kids already on a bus. In only a few pages they are gassed and dumped on the island in short order, so that we can get to the meat of the tale—kids stalking, fighting, and killing other kids. The film version dallies a little longer on actual pedagogy, prefacing the island adventure with a sequence inside the school, in which the teacher (played by Japanese

star actor-director Takeshi Kitano and called, in the movie, "Kitano")
is attacked by a pupil. In the novel, the teacher who briefs the kids,
"Kinpatsu Sakamochi," does so on the island. He is coolly superior,
not above throwing a knife into a child's forehead to underline his
points. Kitano in the film is no less brutal, but he manages to convey
a strange, laid-back *complicity* with the children. He comes over less
as their superior and more as a fellow traveler; he's not a sadistic
authority figure so much as someone who has rather wearily accepted
the violence that is the idiom of the island.

There's another sense in which the novel is a school story, of
course. We go to school to learn things, and the kids in this story
do learn a number of vital lessons. It's just that they're not the kind
of thing usually timetabled as part of a regular school curriculum.
The pedagogy here has to do with the arts of war: how to survive, the
importance of comradeship, when to be ruthless or cautious, when to
attack and when to make alliances, and finally, how to balk the system
and survive. Kids learn this or die.

Cut to real school. Here kids learn the three Rs or—what? Not
die, obviously. Unless of boredom. It's a rare twenty-first-century circumstance in which the ability to parse an irregular French verb or
undertake differential calculus will literally save your life. *Battle Royale*
is a violent, improbable adventure; school a dull and predictable habit
of life. The novel represents not school experience but an exaggerated
fantasia of school experience.

Except I'm going to argue that *Battle Royale* is not a fantasy at all.
Put it in the larger context of school stories and school life and it starts
to seem not a violent outlier, but something far more central.

For much of human history schooling was a minority activity.
The wealthy paid to have their kids educated; the poor put their kids
to work. That changed in the second half of the nineteenth century.
America led the way. The Revolution had placed a particular emphasis
on education—John Adams ringingly announced in 1785 that "the
whole people must take upon themselves the education of the whole
people and be willing to bear the expenses of it. There should not be

a district of one mile square, without a school in it, not founded by a charitable individual, but maintained at the public expense of the people themselves."[1] It took a while, especially in the rural south, for this to actualize itself, but by 1870, all US states provided free elementary schools for their citizens. The US population actually had one of the highest literacy rates at the time. Eighteen seventy was also the year in the UK when the Elementary Education Act finally compelled local authorities to provide schools for all children and compelled all children to attend until they were at least twelve years old. In Japan, the modernization of schooling happened across a similar timeline as part of the so-called "Meiji reforms." In the late 1860s the government sent observers to various Western countries to learn what they could about public education. In 1860 fewer than half of all Japanese children went to school. By 1900, following the institution of local educational boards and Western-style schools all across Japan, more than 90 percent of Japanese children attended school.

School stories reflect this growth. By the twentieth century "going to school" was the norm for most children, and the experience of childhood became inexorably interlinked with the experience of school. "Both sexes are apt to confess," wrote Victorian bluestocking Nancy Hinton, rather primly, in the *Ladies Pocket Magazine* for 1879, "that their happiest days were spent at school. Much truth is expressed in the confession. Past time abstracts the severity from the indulgence; the latter being remembered, brings pleasure into the present cares." This may have been the first time the notion that "school is the happiest time of your life" was put into print, but the sentiment goes back much earlier.

The very first "school story" (indeed, the first full-length novel written for children) was Sarah Fielding's *The Governess, or The Little Female Academy* (1749).[2] Under the benign, loving eye of the teacher, the appropriately named Mrs. Teachum, ten female pupils learn the three *R*s by reading one another stories. At no point do they learn how to disembowel one another with a bowie knife. On the contrary, the emphasis in the novel is that "Love and Affection for each other make the Happiest of all Societies." In her introduction, Fielding declares her aim is to win young readers over to the idea that school can be fun as well as character-forming.

The same moral, though toughed-up for a male rather than female readership, is on display in Thomas Hughes's *Tom Brown's School Days* (1857). Fictional Tom attends the real-life Rugby school, as it had recently been reformed by the real-life Headmaster Thomas Arnold (who also appears in the novel). Arnold believed the primary business of school was in forming a pupil's character; that discipline, hard work, sport, and religion were all necessary parts of this process, and that the subjects taught were important really only insofar as they contributed to this end. It is to Arnold, for instance, that we can trace the notion that schooling should be based upon the study of two dead languages, Latin and Greek. He did countenance the study of modern languages, but in a secondary sense. "I assume it as the foundation of all my view of the case," he confidently declared, "that boys at a public school never will learn to speak or pronounce French well, under any circumstances." It would be enough "if they learn it grammatically as a dead language." No science was taught at Rugby, since Arnold believed it must either take the chief place in the school curriculum, or it must be left out altogether.[3] So it was left out.

This doesn't inconvenience Tom Brown in the least, for he is a boy wholly lacking in book smarts. Because who needs book smarts when you have the soul of a gentleman? Tom is strong, manly, sporty, kind to those weaker than himself, Christian, vigorous. The novel tells us much more about the games of rugby Tom plays than about his classroom lessons. And most of all, Hughes casts school as not so much a venue for intellectual development but rather as an arena for the battle between good and evil.

Evil is represented by the school bully, Flashman, an older boy who has a particular hatred for heroic young Tom:

> Flashman laid wait, and caught Tom before second lesson, and twisted his arm, and went through the other methods of tor-ture in use. "He couldn't make me cry, though," as Tom said

triumphantly to the rest of the rebels; "and I kicked his shins well, I know." And soon it crept out that a lot of the fags were in league, and Flashman excited his associates to join him in bringing the young vagabonds to their senses; and the house was filled with constant chasings, and sieges, and lickings of all sorts; and in return, the bullies' beds were pulled to pieces and drenched with water, and their names written up on the walls with every insulting epithet which the fag invention could furnish. The war, in short, raged fiercely.

(Fags, as you already know, despite your smirks, is nineteenth-century school slang for a younger boy who acts as a sort of unofficial servant for an older boy.) This "war" isn't a million miles from what happens in *Battle Royale*. Nobody gets killed in *Tom Brown*, but it's not for lack of trying on Flashman's part. He literally burns Tom over an open fire and is only prevented from killing him when two boys gang up to attack him:

Flashman was taken aback, and retreated two steps. East looked at Tom. "Shall we try!" said he. "Yes," said Tom desperately. So the two advanced on Flashman, with clenched fists and beating hearts. They were about up to his shoulder, but tough boys of their age, and in perfect training; while he, though strong and big, was in poor condition from his monstrous habit of stuffing and want of exercise. Coward as he was, however, Flashman couldn't swallow such an insult as this; besides, he was confident of having easy work, and so faced the boys, saying, "You impudent young blackguards!" Before he could finish his abuse, they rushed in on him, and began pummelling at all of him which they could reach. He hit out wildly and savagely; but the full force of his blows didn't tell—they were too near to him. It was long odds, though, in point of strength; and in another minute Tom went spinning backwards over a form, and Flashman turned to demolish East with a savage grin.[4]

What's interesting about this is that it is not presented as a lamentable failure of the school authorities, but on the contrary as a necessary part of the manly education of Tom. This is where *Tom Brown's School Days* and *Battle Royale* cross paths. Both understand that what you really learn in school is not the textbook stuff parceled out in the classroom. The real learning happens when kids interact with other kids.

Indeed, it's striking how often nineteenth-century British school stories are built around pupils dying. Look at *Nicholas Nickleby* and *Jane Eyre.* Or look at Dean Farrar's in-its-day extraordinarily popular *Eric, or Little By Little* (1858). Farrar's novel, set in the fictional Rosyln School, tells the story of how lying, smoking, cheating, and (not spelled out in so many words, but unmistakably presented in the novel as the worst of the lot) masturbation lead otherwise good schoolboys "little by little" to ruin and death. Three kids die in that story, including the title character. Victorian writers knew that killing off their innocent childish characters—or even, in the case of *Eric,* their hairy-palmed delinquent childish characters—heightens a novel's pathos marvelously. Modern inheritors of this tradition pluck the same sentimental string. There are so many fatalities of children in the *Harry Potter* books, for instance, it's a wonder the magical equivalent of Her Majesty's Schools Inspectorate hasn't shut Hogwarts down.

It's a small step from the pathos of kids dying to the drama of kids killing. The earliest example of *this* sort of novel is William Golding's *Lord of the Flies* (1954): a school story of a particular kind. Kids abandoned on an island turn by degrees into violent savages and end up murdering one another. Golding, religious in a peculiarly English tortured-but-well-mannered way, thought he was writing a story about Original Sin and the need for Strong Social Structures and Strict Discipline to keep the inner barbarian at bay. Put like that, it makes the novel sound like a kind of bible text of political conservatism, which I suppose is one way of taking it. On the other hand anybody who has read the novel will attest that it doesn't *feel* like that, as a reading experience. I think this is because the crackling energy of the story keeps pulling the novel free of its moralizing origins. Maybe we do identify with Piggy, but that doesn't mean we dislike it when his asthma is mocked or his glasses smashed. We were all kids once; the little savage still lurks within.

It's always struck me as a strange feature of the British education system (I can't speak for other countries) that *Lord of the Flies* has been a staple of assigned school reading for half a century or more. It's almost as if generations of teachers could not help mocking their charges: *Look at all the fun you could be having if it weren't for us and our rules!* And I suppose that's part of the appeal of *Battle Royale* too. Of course, to think about this is to butt our heads against the malign truth at the heart of the human condition—that freedom, though an evident individual and metaphysical good, is a social and religious evil. In an individual sense freedom means self-empowerment and choice; in a social sense it means license, crime, disintegration, and anarchy. Without its rules school would fall apart, and we need our schools to hang together—even if it is those very rules that corrode our individual lives.

Children, who have to deal with all manner of external, adult-imposed rules, internalize a major rule of their own. They call this *fairness*. "It isn't *fair!*" is one of the most vehement ethical statements any child can make. I don't say so in mockery: I hear "It isn't *fair!*" all the time from my kids, and often for trivial reasons, but versions of that same statement, that same outrage, are what powers the moral insights of some of the greatest thinkers in human history. It lies behind the writings of Marx and Gandhi, and the preaching of Christ.

Suzanne Collins's mega-selling *The Hunger Games* (2008) makes an interesting parallel case to *Battle Royale* in this context. Collins insists, and I am too much of a gentleman to doubt her word, that she had not so much as heard of Koushun Takami's novel until *after* the first novel of her *Hunger Games* trilogy had already been delivered to the publishers. But putting the question of direct influence aside, there is a crucial difference of *emphasis* in the way the novels (and films) represent their children. Katniss Everdeen, Collins's heroine, is a good person. She willingly sacrifices herself to spare her younger sister, Prim, the terror and death of being picked for the games. We root for her and identify with her, and Collins is careful not to have her act meanly or with cruelty, or in some other way that might compromise our sympathy for her. She has (through no fault of her own) been placed in this kill-or-be-killed situation! Nice girls finish last, and we don't want that. Sacrificing herself in order to take her sister's place is one thing; sacrificing her life in order not to be guilty of murder would make her a victim, and America despises a victim. So Collins plays it the only way she can: Katniss in the arena tries to keep out of the way of the "bad" kids who are eagerly killing the others. She protects a weaker contestant, Rue, even though Rue and she are notionally rivals. Then one of the bad kids kills Rue, which legitimizes Katniss killing the killer. We, as readers, get to have our cake and eat it too—we get the vicarious thrill of breaking the rules and venting our repressed anger in murderous violence, and we get to retain our sense of ourselves as above such savagery. It is, in other words, a kind of cheat, ethically speaking.

One of the things that makes *Battle Royale* so fascinating is the way it refuses this ethical narrative. Its characters are nice and nasty, pampered or damaged, as real kids are—and we root for some more than others. But the story itself is both more arbitrarily conceived and more shocking for it. In Koushun Takami's world, things *aren't* fair. Late in the novel, responding to a complaint that *it's not fair* ("A government is supposed to serve the needs of the people! We shouldn't be slaves to our own system. If you think this country makes sense, you're totally insane!") Sakamochi, the teacher, dismissively says:

> You're still a kid . . . This is a marvelous country. It's the most
> prosperous country in the world . . . The thing is though, this
> prosperity only comes as a result of unifying the population with
> a powerful government at the center. A certain degree of control
> is always necessary. (559)

"You're still a kid" almost makes it look like a moral is being presented to us. If you think life is fair, you need to grow up. If you think childhood is innocent play and singing pretty songs you're a fool.

The weird, disturbing force of *Battle Royale* clearly has something to do with innocence being violated. The thought of a maniac taking a gun into a school and shooting a crowd of cowering kids naturally upsets us much more than the thought of soldiers shooting one another on the battlefield. This latter, if we're honest, rather excites us. Certainly it excites us in story form. War stories have been a staple of world culture since the *Iliad,* and earlier. There is no equivalent literary genre based on Columbine-style school shootings. The proper reaction to a tragedy like that is grief and moral revulsion. Yet it's precisely this that makes Koushun Takami's novel so arresting—that it treats the latter like the former. School, it says, *is* war. Almost anyone who has been to school can feel the emotional truth of that.

The idea that children are somehow "innocent" and that this innocence is somehow excellent, holy, and worth protecting is an invention of a particular historical moment, at the end of the eighteenth century. Before that the Western consensus was that children were born into original sin, their souls marked and shaped by Adam's fall. People, mostly, thought of children not as innocent but as very specifically guilty, and the business of *caring* for children was largely a matter of curbing their "natural" instincts to mischief, wickedness, and harm. To spare the rod was to spoil the child.

Romanticism changed all that. First the French philosopher Jean-Jacques Rousseau made a big splash by repudiating the very notion of "original sin": *"Tout est bien sortant des mains de l'Auteur des choses,"* he wrote in his extraordinarily influential novel of childhood and schooling, *Émile, or On Education* (1762); *"Tout dégénère entre les mains de l'homme."* Everything that leaves the hands of the Creator of the World is *good.* It is men who corrupt it. Elsewhere in the novel Rousseau pours out gouts of pure syrup in his praise of childish innocence.

Love childhood, indulge its sports, its pleasures, its delightful instincts. Who has not sometimes regretted that age when laughter was ever on the lips, and when the heart was ever at peace? Why rob these innocents of the joys which pass so quickly, of that precious gift which they cannot abuse? Why fill with bitterness the fleeting days of early childhood, days which will no more return for them than for you?

These words fell on receptive ears. For Romantics, the "child" became the locus for a holy innocence. William Blake makes children the absolute symbol of all that is untainted, pure, and spiritual. His *Songs of Innocence* (1794) are full of this kind of thing:

> On a cloud I saw a child,
> And he laughing said to me:
> "Pipe a song about a Lamb."
> So I piped with merry cheer;
> "Piper, pipe that song again."
> So I piped; he wept to hear.

"White as an angel is the English child!" was how he put it in another poem. Now, I love Blake with a great love, but speaking as a father of two English children I have to wonder—had he ever actually *met* a child? He himself had neither sons nor daughters. You don't have to believe in original sin to recognize that childhood has the capacity for wickedness. Even the most perfunctory of observation tells us that children are far more likely to bicker and fight than sit placidly on a cloud piping merry cheer.

Nonetheless this notion that children embody a special, even a holy innocence has shown extraordinary staying power. For many people the idea that children possess "innocence" still carries great force. How else does a book like *Battle Royale* still shock readers? It is the dissonance between the innocence of children and the very un-innocent things they are compelled to do that unsettles us.

This sense of a corrupting world degrading the innocence of children applies at more than the individual level. How many people believe that a malign event like the Columbine school shooting was actually a symptom of our modern degraded society? Pick your bugbear, whichever pet theory you prefer as a corrupting agent. Children *are* innocent, but rock music (or rap music, or television, or the Internet, or the sexual revolution of the 1960s, or socialism, or fluoride in the water, or the presence of guns, or the *absence* of guns) has corrupted them such that they now dress in black hoodies, play *Doom,* and walk into their schools carrying automatic weapons.

When Koushun Takami published his book in 1999 he looked to be tapping into a uniquely modern manifestation of our degraded contemporary life. Nineteen ninety-nine was the year of the Columbine shooting, after all. It didn't *use* to be like that in schools. Did it?

Yesterday at noon a boy sixteen years of age was shot by his brother. He was a member of the High School of this city and was, we are told, something over the average good boy of Los Angeles. This boy lost his life through the too common habit among boys of carrying deadly weapons. We do not know that this habit can be broken up. We do not know that school teachers have the right, or would exercise it if they had, of searching the pockets of their pupils, but it seems almost a necessity that some such rule be enforced. The hills west of town are not safe for pedestrians after school hours. Nearly every school-boy carries a pistol, and the power of these pistols range from the harmless six-bit auction concern to the deadly Colt's six-shooter.[5]

Ah, but surely *that* was accidental, wasn't it? Children don't actually go to school to fight and kill one another.

Except maybe for Will Guess. On June 12, 1887, in Cleveland, Tennessee, young Will Guess took a revolver with him to his school. During a lesson he used the gun to shoot dead the teacher, Miss Irene Fann. He explained his motives afterward: one day earlier, Miss Fann had caned his sister. Oh: and Ben Corbery. On April 24, 1890, at the Meridian Street School in Brazil, Indiana, the children were playing during break time when Corbery drew a pistol and shot ten-year-old Cora Brubach in the face. He did so because Cora had "told" on Ben to a teacher. Then there were the events of December 13, 1898, when a group of youngsters became rowdy during a student's performance at the school exhibition at Charles Town, West Virginia. The teacher, Mr. Fisher, attempted to eject them from the school. They resisted, and other people in the audience came to Fisher's aid. A fight broke out. A boy named Harry Flasher was shot in the heart and killed; a youth named Henry Carney was fatally shot in the spine, Ralph Jones was shot and killed, and two others died. Several others were wounded. On March 11, 1908, at the Laurens School, a finishing school in Boston, Massachusetts, Sarah Chamberlain Weed shot Elizabeth Bailey Hardee to death, afterward using the same gun to commit suicide. On May 18, 1927, at Bath School, in Bath, Michigan, Andrew Kehoe, the school treasurer (having previously murdered his wife) detonated a large quantity of dynamite in the basement of the school, killing forty-five people, almost all of them children. On May 28, 1931, at a school in Duluth, Minnesota, a pupil brought a pistol to class and used it to shoot and kill his teacher, twenty-four-year-old Katherine McMillen. On September 24, 1937, in Toledo, Ohio, twelve-year-old Robert Snyder went into the office of the school principal, June Mapes, and asked her to call one of Snyder's classmates. When she refused to do this Snyder shot her dead. He fled school grounds and was later shot by the police. On June 26, 1946, in Brooklyn, New York, at the Brooklyn High School for Automotive Trades, a gang of seven teenagers insisted that one fifteen-year-old boy hand over his pocket money. When the boy refused he was shot in the chest. April 9, 1952: New York City. A teacher insisted that a fifteen-year-old boarding school student surrender certain pinup images of women in bathing suits. Rather than do so, the pupil shot the teacher dead. October 2, 1953, in Chicago, Illinois. Fourteen-year-old Patrick Colletta asked Bernice Turner, also fourteen, out on a date in front of the class. When she turned him down, he handed her a pistol and dared her to fire it at him, telling her "it is only a toy." Turner's shot killed Colletta. On October 20, 1956, in the Booker T. Washington Junior High School in New York, a student was wounded in the forearm by another student armed with a homemade firearm. On October 2, 1957, again in New York City, a sixteen-year-old schoolboy was shot in the leg by a fifteen-year-old classmate. On May 1, 1958, in Massapequa, Long Island, a fifteen-year-old high school student was shot and killed in the school toilets by a classmate. On October 17, 1961, at Morey Junior High School in Denver, Colorado, a fourteen-year-old school student called Tennyson Beard had an argument with fifteen-year-old William Hachmeister. Beard drew a revolver and fired repeatedly. Hachmeister was wounded, but one bullet hit fourteen-year-old Deborah Faith Humphrey, killing her. December 30, 1974, in Olean, a city in western New York, seventeen-year-old Anthony Barbaro brought a rifle and shotgun to school, killing three and wounding eleven. On February 18, 1975, at the Marist College in Poughkeepsie, Shelley Lynn Sperling was shot dead in the cafeteria by a boy she had refused to date. Then there's the case of the son of President Lyndon B. Johnson's press secretary, George Christian. John Daniel Christian went to school in Austin, Texas. On May 18, 1978, the then thirteen-year-old John Daniel brought his father's .22 rifle to school and used it to kill his English teacher. Christian was never prosecuted. After two years in a psychiatric institution, he recovered and is now a practicing attorney in Austin.

These are a tiny fraction of cases in the US alone, and we're not even out of the 1970s. Delve for even a little time into the history of school shootings and it starts to dawn on you—*Battle Royale* isn't satire, or dark fable, or fantastical extrapolation. *Battle Royale* is realism. It is a novel that makes manifest one of the great secrets of school life, a secret that has been latent in the long traditions of school literature. School is about the interaction of Flashman on the one hand and Piggy on the other. School is about many things, but one of the things it is about is violence.

There's a good reason for this—violence is not a thing in itself. Violence is a mode of interacting with other people, a way of physically articulating our feelings about other people. Without the structure of those feelings, the representation of violence becomes merely baffling, or disgusting. Only with them can it make sense. And the truly crucial thing about school is not the curriculum; it is that this is where all our peers are: our friends and enemies, the people we have desperate secret crushes upon, the people who bully us, the people we admire or despise. School gives us what the family is too small to give us: our first proper sample-size model for human interaction. If you think that *Battle Royale* is just a pretext for portraying a lot of violent acts performed, kinkily, by youngsters, you're wrong. In common with the larger tradition of school stories, it is about the forty-two characters and the ways in which they interact with one another, and the point of the violence is to highlight the extreme nature and emotional intensity of those interactions. It is about school. For some, school may be the happiest time of your life. For others, though, school can be murder.

ENDNOTES

1. John Adams, letter to John Jebb, September 10, 1785. Richard Alan Ryerson et al (eds), *The Adams Papers: Adams Family Correspondence,* Volume 6 (Harvard Univ. Press, 1992), 5:540.

2. There are earlier books about schooling, containing suggestions as to how to educate children—for example the anonymous *L'Ecole des Filles* (Paris, 1658). But Fielding's appears to be the first specifically fictional account of the process.

3. Arnold's opinion is quoted from T. W. Bamford (ed), *Thomas Arnold on Education* (Cambridge University Press, 1970), 116. He also insisted that "rather than have science the principal thing in my son's mind, I would gladly have him think the sun went round the earth, and that the stars were so many spangles set in the bright blue firmament. Surely the one thing needful for a Christian and an English man to study is Christian, moral, and political philosophy."

4. Thomas Hughes, *Tom Brown's School Days* (1857), 184. This is from Chapter 9, "A Chapter of Accidents."

5. *Los Angeles Herald,* September 11, 1874.

Innocence Lost and Regained: Bradbury, Takami, and the Cult of the Child

BY KATHLEEN MILLER

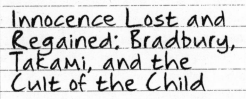

Children are brats. Just ask any parent. They can be absolute monsters. Perhaps it's no small wonder, then, that some believe they should be seen and not heard—but I would venture to go further and state outright that, contrary to popular belief, children simply don't exist. At least, not in the way that we think they do.

Childhood—or that bygone, innocent state that we understand ourselves to have experienced—is a cherished myth, a fiction, a farce. Aided and abetted by elaborate constructions of fantasy and dreaming, the image of the child is promulgated through the elaborate cultural industry of Children's Literature (and more recently these days, the plastic taffy of Young Adult fare), a racket orchestrated by adults who might as well be giants from a child's perspective. Interestingly enough, it's the adults (supposed "former" children themselves) who buy (and censor) the books for the kiddies in the first place. Like the proverbial piggyback ride, the old conceit of being unable to see without standing on the shoulders of giants is in turn crystallized into something far more sinister. Adult and child alike are only capable of seeing in effect what it is adults want them to see. Something that is thus, unavoidably and inescapably, *adult.* Consider it a game of peekaboo in reverse—absent presences that hound, and in doing so, howl volumes.

As Agent Mulder would have it, the truth is out there, presented in varying forms and fads over the years: the behavioral development of infancy and adolescence given to all manners of lurid sexual proclivity courtesy of Piaget and Freud, alongside the glittering debris of the shattered Lacanian mirror stage of self and Other, whose fragments continue to be pored over by generations of theorists like some twisted jigsaw puzzle. Combing through the cultural debris of what thinkers like Lee Edelman have proclaimed the cult of the Child, I turn to two particular puzzle-builders, poets and prophets in their own right—Ray Bradbury and Koushun Takami. Though oceans and decades apart, both writers devilishly remind us that amidst the stomping grounds of childhood there is more than meets the eye, and that the "I" is invariably a rather complicated creature.

For one thing, there is always this seeming sense that one possesses a child within—an inner child. A child that never forgets that you have abandoned and forgotten him, like a shopping bag at the mall, left on some lonely bench, lost—and never quite found again, save in faded photographs and pairs of too-small swimming trunks. The hazy face on the milk cartons of yesteryear haunts us like a missing person report every time we are forced to confront the changing shape of ourselves and that stranger aging daily in the mirror's cold confines. "Have you seen me lately?" it inquires. Summer and the thrill of brand-new sneakers and dandelion wine were all only yesterday, melted into the creases of the mind like late afternoon ice cream. Where *did* it all go? *Farewell Summer,* writes Bradbury, trying to recapture the dregs of his past with pent-up longing. Yet for all our urges and aspirations to "live forever," nothing can ever really stay.

Takami would instead point us toward a stickier substance far less vanilla in nature. We have only to turn to the thick clotting and congealing bath of blood that stains and saturates the traumatic pages of *Battle Royale,* whose nightmarish premise is strangely catastrophic and yet comical in its violent excesses. Children killing children? The idea of it is not nearly so horrifying as the fact that it actually proceeds to play out in grand, self-fulfilling fashion—collapsing all preconceived convictions that kids are pure at heart, incapable of brutally acting out in such a vacuum without the corrupting influence of the *Adult* with a capital, scarlet "A." Of course some kids are more than willing. While Shuya and Noriko provide us with valiant holdouts for hope, it's the kids like Mitsuko and Kazuo who really salt the flesh of the story, so to speak. Mitsuko is famously forged in part by parental neglect and abuse, but also by fierce self-rule. Both acknowledging and embracing the chaos of her freefall spiral into triumphant degeneracy, she wields the empty shell of her past like a weapon, exploiting others with a calculated poise bordering on that of artful grace. Kazuo's saving grace in turn—if not perversion—is a damage concealed even from himself, from the splinter digging into his skull, to the deaths of all those close to him.

With so much predicated upon a past series of unspoken events, Kazuo is a deadly poster child for the entangled horror of nature and absent nurturing running wild. Though he fits the prototypical orphan mold like Shuya, the splinter element in Kazuo's case points to a deeper-set damage that is even more engrained—that sliver or fissure within the cultural consciousness that we all too often fail to even apprehend let alone question. Just as Kazuo's father and the doctor attempt (and fail) to tend to Kazuo, in seeking to heal and protect the Legion of the Child on a broader level, we as readers wound and further stave off our ability to really feel and acknowledge the reality of that child in the first place.

By cordoning off the experience of what it means to be a child under so many layers of censorship labels and ratings boards, developmental milestones and core-curricula, we lose sight of what is seemingly being preserved. It's a queer project, really, given that efforts to suspend the childhood state are not meant to meet with enduring success—just look at the disdain showered upon new generations of adults still caught in varying stages of arrested development. Sheltering the child only leads to further suffering in Bradbury's works as well. Take the unfortunate case of Mr. Charles Underhill in Bradbury's short story "The Playground," who in an effort to shield his fragile son Jim from the calcified violence of the schoolyard makes a Faustian bargain in which he takes his son's place for an eternity. Mayday! Mayday! See: helicopter parenting gone wrong.

The idea "of someone else having so much control" over you is an "entirely revolting" concept for determinedly self-reliant characters like Shinji to swallow (327). Yet even those who opt for the tough love approach and teach kids to be self-reliant and grow up fast and trust no one, are still sheltering, in a sense. A thick skin developed prematurely can blunt the discovery of the individual on their own terms in learning how to come to trust in themselves and others—like the trust of Shuya and Noriko in Shogo and each other that proves their saving grace. While part of this trust may stem from naïveté, much of it still entails a calculated fall. Yumiko, one of the well-intentioned-but-unfortunately-executed minds behind the megaphone-appeal-turned-massacre, voices the innate need to find grounding in others: "I want to trust people. If I can't then everything falls apart" (138).

No trust, no future? Again, we really have to still wonder about the fact that so much of growing up is founded upon a precarious and yet necessary mixture of trust and innocence; a willing *suspension of disbelief,* if you will—and the threat of it being invoked for the wrong reasons, for games more dangerous and far beyond mere fiction. The childish capacity for imagination is turned on its head and epitomized for Shuya in "that moment back there when he first realized someone was willing to play" (66). A fundamental component of all this comes down to the underlying power of fiction and stories and dreaming (it's not for nothing that Shuya's best subject is literature); the continual dance around the open-ended space of origins and beginnings from which we construct ourselves and each other. And much like in the game, language emerges as the very collar at the binding center of it all, which chokes and yet watches and listens to us the whole time. That both makes us and breaks us. See: the bullets that ricochet like the keys of an old manual typewriter, "a mildly pleasant rattling sound" (82).

Nothing is perhaps more riveting, then, than the spectacle of revealing and reveling in the fantasy of the Child collapsing in upon itself. It is this collapse that forms the basis of a similar fantasy echoed earlier on in Bradbury's darker works. The children of Bradbury's stories are by turns cunning and clever and curious beyond measure. They are named things like Tom and Will and Douglas. And all too often, they are prescient creatures wise beyond their years. There is the "Small Assassin"—a preternatural infant with murderous intent, seeking vengeance upon its parental unit years before *Rosemary's Baby* was even conceived. There is also the tragic figure of Margot, locked in a closet by her cruel classmates, left to wither away from the brief burst of sun after seven years of Venusian rain in "All Summer in a Day." More heartbreaking than their malicious actions is her ominous silence from behind the locked door.

And then there are Peter and Wendy—the aptly named offspring of *Peter Pan* and the Lost Boys who murder their parents in the oven-baked sunny savannah of "The Veldt," a virtual reality playroom mysteriously brought to life by a child's dreaming; death ignited by imagination. See: *Fahrenheit 451.* Also see: death by lion-mauling. Bloody stuff—but the kind of meat that makes you smack your lips with dark delight and hungry glee, perhaps to stick it to the parents who wouldn't let you eat chocolate syrup for dinner and stay up past your bedtime and read authors like Anne Rice and Stephen King. That serves them right!

Right?

You have to admit that these kinds of children operate on some troubling level beyond the sour humor of curdled fairy tale. Clearly, the kids are not all right. This is in part due to the fleeting and fictitious nature of childhood itself—this perpetually retrospective state that one views in hindsight: "When I became a man I put away such childish things." The kids are not all right because a) they are not *all* right (no one is, at heart—just ask Thomas Hobbes) and b) it ain't *right* to force them into being kids in the first place. Just like the idea of forcing an ax into a teenager's hands and telling him to hack his friends to death or else die himself sounds ludicrous and unnatural, so too the proclamation that "kids will be kids" (or as adults are so fond of saying of adolescents in later stages, "It's just a phase.") Life is, after all, something of continual progression and change, but still a *contained* entity; you carry the entirety of it with you. There aren't separate chapters—like a wet paperback, the ink and words bleed together, swell and overflow. One could say that in Bradbury's case, it is worth trying to swim against the ravaging currents of time to reconnect with your former selves in a warm bath of remembrance. But of course, the water grows far darker the further out you swim, the depths murky with hidden trauma and fictions of remembering.

As Margarida Morgado notes in exploring child disappearance narratives, "children are made prisoners of fictions of innocence" (246). Weaponized and idealized by the very virtue and vulnerability ascribed to them, the figure of the child becomes an instrument for authority, and the excess of dismantling and shattering of something so seemingly fragile and young is conventionally regarded with horror. Which is exactly what makes Takami's work so brilliant. He explodes the empty center at the heart of it all and the false ideals of blameless youth we have erected to bulwark the machinations of social order. Much of this revelation is conveyed through the shrapnel of blurred contrast: Shuya using his baseball skills to catch a hand grenade; Kaori handling her gun "like a kid playing with a water pistol" (267). It also operates in reverse—the card autographed by the Great Dictator and given to the "winner" of each class "looked like some kid scribbled on it" (170). These kinds of juxtapositions capture the wonderful unraveling and reorientation of things. For try as we might to cover up the chaos, whether it's the madness of a fascist state, child abuse, or growing pains, there is no division between child and adult, no "before" and "after" when it comes to innocence tarnished and lost. Rather, it all exists on a continuum—and the construct of childhood, especially, only in a retrospective dimension, after the fact, as something longed for and lost.

What, then, might yet be regained? It's important to note that Bradbury's conceit of the Veldt itself as a nursery—a place of life intended to nurture—plays double-duty as an abject, uncut wilderness. Savage, open, untamed, its verdant expanses crested with continuous waves of heat and burning, when left to its own devices, this fallow space proves strangely overripe and dangerous in its fecund ground-swell of anger and emotion—a distant rumble on the horizon, a sound of thunder. And most telling of all, a space born out of metal, plastic, artificial, mechanical—and *inhabited by young minds*. While the children in *Battle Royale* are driven from one grid of terrain to another by foreboding adult overlords, and for the most part turn upon each other, Bradbury's nursery-dwelling youngsters terraform their own gridded hologram cell to entrap the very authority figures who would bring about the playroom's end with a flick of the OFF switch. Originally published as "The World the Children Made," his cautionary tale evokes the darkest side of a desire gilded in childish imagining that can be boiled down to the source of the word itself. Stemming from the Dutch and German root "veld," *velt* emerges from the warlike space of "field of battle"—and it is so in grand, martial fashion that we must embrace the bloodlust of the *Battle Royale,* pitting our many past and present selves against a younger self ever older beyond years. For just as no man is an island, it has always been a contest of us versus them, of past and present brawling it out for a future imperfect.

A key component of this struggle, in turn, is the ability to reimagine possibilities of what was and could still be, without becoming completely delusional in the process. Mizuho Inada is as psychotic as Kazuo when living out her mission as space warrior Prexia Dikianne Mizuho—occupying a strategic defense mechanism of rich fantasy which itself is still no match for its polar opposite: a calculating mind of pure instinct and raw brutality. Such fictions, it seems, can at times prove *too* effective: the mind can take us very far in sealing ourselves off from the real world, but also to the brink, and past all love, feeling, and reason. Enveloped in makeshift shelters of creation, we risk losing our minds like poor Kaori, whose fangirl obsessions end in a miniature tableaux in which the pop-icon locket around her neck "looked like an island in a lake of blood" (269). The very island itself, the site of battle, scaled down to sinisterly pint-sized dimensions—a potent crystallization of inner dreaming and bitter realities in which the continual wringing-out of self and soul that causes us to turn upon each other from the inside out is made manifest.

For least of all things, the island is contained space. As bodies pile up, we are continually re-confronted with them and the topsy-turvy nature of the forces behind their accumulation. In the Nursery of the Mind, we can wipe the slate clean and start all over again, and again, and again, rebuilding a world mechanically sanitized and yet populated by our own wicked imaginings. And it's there, in the loopholes—the rabbit holes, the leap-spaces, the drift, whatever you want to call it—in these liminal side alleys and bleeds and margins and gutters, where the hope of escape beckons. In the white behind the words, we can still dance free, the closest space to a tarnished innocence bordering dream realms and nightmare, and not unlike the drug-induced, sleepy transition into the blood-soaked fields of *Battle Royale*, where the game becomes its own salvation.

According to Bradbury, children are the rare creatures that can see through the masks we sculpt for ourselves to hide behind. Whether it's the gas masks on the school bus or our pretense to ourselves that reading a book like *Battle Royale* is just harmless escapism anyway, at some point we must own up to the responsibility of having opened and turned the page in the first place, caught between guilty hunger and a child's gaze. In this sense, the fiction of their existence is a thrilling truth made crystal clear through death-rimmed revelry. Their fascination with violence, with destruction—and anyone who has ever watched children crush any number of insects or topple block towers can attest—bespeaks minds that are in fact far from naïve, highly attuned and perceptive to the nuances that abound. Though they are often cast as "impressionable," and open to a variety of dimensions, it is not so much an innocence that they possess as it is a willingness to observe and confront all angles of a situation, to consider and spectate and *play* with different modes. And most importantly, to take the instruments and parameters of the game with which they are presented and use it against itself.

From *Battle Royale* to the calculating children in Bradbury's tales who are all too aware of the chinks in adult armor when it comes to how kids are perceived, it is by exploiting parental blindness and naïveté that they are able to rewrite the fictions that enchain them. In Takami's story, quite literally so: the very pencil the students are forced to use to write "We will kill" is ultimately repurposed as the instrument of Sakamochi's death at the hands of Shogo. Childhood is exposed for the malleable bomb that it is through creation rebelling against its master; Humpty Dumpty smashed to yolky pulp for all to see, a martyr to the cause. Though we have created these worlds for them, the islands meant to protect them (from themselves, or ourselves, or something still far darker) have proven prisons, overrun with creepers and vines and swaying branches, "cutting them off completely from the blue sky," and from the sun (290). And they are now building their own worlds to house us in turn, as they become our keepers.

Never put away such childish things; for without them we are indeed left with a "glass, darkly," these dark lenses for viewing—wonderfully gruesome, dark horror shows like *A Clockwork Orange* and *Something Wicked This Way Comes* and *Battle Royale*. And through these grisly spectacles of man and mind, come to better know, and be known.

WORKS CITED

Morgado, Margarida. "A Loss Beyond Imagining: Child Disappearance in Fiction." The Yearbook of English Studies, Vol. 32, Children in Literature (2002), pp. 244-259. Modern Humanities Research Association. http://www.jstor.org/stable/3509061. Accessed: 18/06/2013

Takami, Koushun, *Battle Royale: The Novel*. Translated by Yuji Oniki. San Francisco: Haikasoru, 2009.

From Dangerous to Desirable: *Battle Royale* and the Gendering of Youth Culture

BY RAECHEL DUMAS

"Shuya couldn't die," thinks Noriko. "Because Shuya was like a holy man with a guitar. He was always kind to everyone, and he was always so sympathetic to the sorrows of others. But he would never lose that powerful smile. He was so upright and transparent and innocent, but also tough. *He's like my guardian angel. How could someone like that die?*" (Takami 380). Noriko's description of Shuya departs considerably from popular perceptions of Japanese youth culture in the period surrounding *Battle Royale*'s 1999 publication. During the 1990s terms such as *gakkyū hōkai* (classroom collapse) became increasingly commonplace in Japan, where the nation's youth served as a scapegoat for the displacement of anxieties concerning the possibility of cultural collapse. *BR* approaches this dialogue critically, drawing attention to Japan's neoconservative libels against youth culture and the supposed breakdown of values held dear by proponents of Japanese nationalism. In doing so, it resituates the responsibility for the perceived damage inflicted upon post-bubble Japan's national psyche onto the shoulders of the government itself. The collapse of the Battle Royale Program at the hands of the novel's youth is one of the work's most universally gratifying components. Yet considered within a specifically Japanese cultural framework, a second dimension of the novel's pleasure also comes to light. While on the one hand *BR*'s heroic survivors Shuya and Noriko challenge perceptions of the dangers of youth, on the other, they do so by affirming a second set of questionable social constructs: the widespread, heavily idealized images of masculinity and femininity that saturated the 1990s Japanese media sphere.

On the surface, Shuya is an embodiment of characteristics common to the protagonists of *shōnen* (boys') and *seinen* (young men's) manga. Shōnen manga, exemplified by titles such as *Dragon Ball, One Piece, Inuyasha,* and *Fullmetal Alchemist* (to name but a few internationally popular works), is geared toward school-aged boys and has historically concerned itself with depicting archetypal male heroism across a diverse array of genres. Seinen manga, which is often more explicitly violent than shōnen, targets adult male audiences, is equally (if not more) oriented around male activity, and includes such titles as *Akira* and *Berserk,* along with the manga version of *BR.*

While shōnen and seinen heroes cannot be reduced to a static set of traits—creators have gone to great, and sometimes supernatural, lengths to diversify them—they do embody certain qualities that identify them as the types of characters audiences have come to demand over the course of decades. Shōnen protagonists—think *Dragonball*'s Goku and *Inuyasha*'s eternally youthful title character—are typically junior high to high school-aged, possess eccentric qualities or interests that differentiate them from their peers, are cast as ardent defenders of the community, and undergo personal growth in the process of overcoming physical challenges. The seinen protagonist likewise possesses one or more exceptional qualities that set him apart and, like *Akira*'s bad boy biker Kaneda and *Berserk*'s Guts, finds himself faced with transformative adversity.

Shuya is situated within a long lineage of such protagonists, many of whom, like him, are engaged in subversive activities. Our hero's justice-oriented motives and willingness to challenge dominant ideologies call to mind the struggles of a long list of heavily principled manga and anime figures that precede him—among them *Fist of the North Star*'s anti-authoritarian Kenshirō, who dedicates himself to protecting the weak; *Dragon Ball*'s Goku, who turns on his own race to defend Earth; and *Akira*'s Kaneda, bent on the destruction of a corrupt post-apocalyptic government.

Considered within the rhetorical framework surrounding youth culture in 1990s Japan, Shuya's resemblance to some of the nation's most famed subversive protagonists gives rise to a crucial question: in a society obsessed with the negative potentialities located in childhood, does Shuya—"the one with dangerous ideas" (33)—not constitute further evidence of the perils of youth culture? Were Shuya merely a reproduction of conventional male protagonists, the answer would be a resounding "Yes." But a closer look at this character illustrates that he is also aligned with a relatively new image of masculinity that departs from the socially disruptive heroes that are presented throughout Japan's long history of popular narratives.

Shuya represents a character type that in the 1970s began to emerge within a different sector of the manga sphere, and which by the time of *BR*'s publication had come to constitute an alternative, and highly desirable, figuration of Japanese masculinity. The 1970s witnessed a diversification of *shōjo* (girls') manga, which over the course of the next several decades would give birth to an alternative image of the masculine ideal. As reflected by contemporary titles such as *Antique Bakery* and *Princess, Princess,* these new storylines celebrate male characters presenting nontraditional attributes, including so-called "feminine" physical features and interests, emotional sensitivity, and homosocial and homoerotic desire. In the 1980s, and partially in response to the second-wave feminist movement, alternative constructions of masculinity began to appear across Japan's mainstream media sphere as well. These new men saturated daytime television dramas, musical stages, and other consumer spaces catering predominately to female audiences. Their appeal was likewise located in their ambiguous physical attributes, sensitivity to gender issues, and capacity to take on both traditionally masculine and feminine roles.

Shuya's identification with this alternative formulation of masculinity is most evident in his relationship with Noriko, who wins his heart by virtue of her ability to pacify Shuya's "knee-jerk" rage with her soothing expressions of optimism concerning the possibility of socio-political change (207). The narrator highlights Shuya's sense of devotion to Noriko at multiple junctures, beginning with the death of his best friend, Yoshitoki. In a moment that emphasizes Shuya's ever-lasting commitment to Yoshitoki and sensitivity to Noriko's plight, Shuya becomes fixated on a single motivation for survival: *"Come on, my best friend had a crush on you,"* he thinks as he and Noriko survey their situation. *"So if I'm going to help anyone, it's got to be you, no matter what"* (69).

Shuya's actions are driven by a largely maternal sense of obligation toward Noriko. This is not to say that Shuya, like Japan's new men, does not exhibit behaviors consistent with paternal figures as well—however, his unhesitating willingness to acknowledge female experience and insight complicates readings of his character as traditionally paternalistic. Moreover, drawing on the immense popularity of Japanese television characters embodying more fluid masculinities— for instance, *Long Vacation*'s Hidetoshi Sena—the text makes an explicit reference to the parallel between Shuya and Noriko's evolving relationship and the romantic plotlines that, by the time of the novel's publication, had come to saturate Japanese daytime television pro-grams geared toward female audiences: "I was all right about the two main characters ending up together," Sakura explains to her boyfriend Kazuhiko as they discuss the most recent episode of the nighttime soap opera *Tonight, at the Same Place.* "That's how it's supposed to be" (87).

Shuya's ability to straddle the borders of masculinity and femi-ninity is also emphasized in descriptions of his musical talents and physical appearance. In one scene, Megumi reflects upon some of Shuya's most extraordinary qualities, focusing on his neutrally pitched voice, "unfamiliar" rhythms, and hairstyle. These features grant Shuya an appeal that aligns closely with that of the sensitive male charac-ters of shōjo manga and anime and the types of men who came to grace Japanese television screens, musical stages, and youth-oriented magazines from the 1980s onward. Significantly, although Shuya's confession that his hairstyle is inspired by Springsteen is lost on Megumi, the teen's long, permed locks are meaningful within a specifically Japanese cultural context. A popular style among a number of male pop stars that have dominated Japanese idol culture since the 1990s—SMAP's Gorō Inagaki and several members of Arashi, to name just a few—the shoulder-length perm is a notable component of the contemporary *bishōnen* (beautiful young boy) aesthetic. The narrator further emphasizes Shuya's beauty via repeated references to his double eyelids, a highly sought-after feature among many Japanese women—in fact, double eyelid surgery is the most common form of cosmetic surgery among women in many parts of East Asia.

Shuya is further romanticized through his obsession with Springsteen, an American rock star who represents that which Shuya's country has abandoned. Yet while Shuya's affinity with Springsteen serves on the one hand to symbolize the youth's political radicalism, on the other it functions as another mode of emphasizing our hero's ostensibly more feminine traits. Shuya's Springsteen song of choice is the 1975 hit "Born to Run," whose coming-of-age narrative draws attention to the novel's own emphasis on the transition from childhood to adult subjectivity. The lyrics also reflect a psychology often attributed to Japan's new men, with the speaker professing his own emotional sensitivity. Shuya persistently adopts Springsteen's composition to express his own desire to leave Japan behind; perhaps the most memorable co-optation of the singer's lyrics, however, is located on the final page of the novel, wherein the song becomes an expression of Shuya's fierce devotion to Noriko: *"Together Noriko we'll live with the sadness,"* he thinks. *"I'll love you with all the madness in my soul"* (576).

For the purpose of better understanding how Shuya's persona is framed largely against, rather than within the confines of, figurations of masculinity that ostensibly pose a threat to the existing social order, it is useful to consider Takami's depiction of his nemeses, Program administrator Kinpatsu Sakamochi and cold-blooded killer Kazuo Kiriyama. Sakamochi's given name derives from the title character of the television drama series *Kinpachi Sensei,* which first aired in 1979. The allusion is tongue-in-cheek—the show's Kinpachi Sakamoto represents an upstanding role model for the various troubled youth that appear throughout the series—and the text itself helpfully draws attention to its own satirical use of the allusion: "Kinpatsu Sakamochi? Was this some kind of joke? Given the situation, maybe it was a pseudonym" (22).

A closer look at Sakamochi reveals a somewhat less humorous play on broader media trends. "What stuck out most though was the man's hairstyle," Shuya observes. "He wore it down to his shoulders like a woman in her prime. It reminded Shuya of the grainy Xeroxed cover of a Joan Baez tape he'd bought on the black market" (21). Desirable images of male androgyny within Japan are diverse, ranging from the ubiquitous youth featured in daytime dramas and boy bands to highly specific character types that appear across the spectrum of boy-love manga. However, the operative word here is "boy," which signifies youthfulness despite the sometimes-murky distinction between childhood and adulthood within Japanese visual culture. By contrast, Sakamochi's appearance disallows his identification with Shuya and other popular male objects of female fantasy, for as a decidedly adult man who resembles that which he is decidedly not— a mature American woman—he exists outside of the established bounds of desirability.

Shuya's meditation on Sakamochi's unsettling appearance is a mere preface to the revelation of the man's sadistic inclinations toward rape and murder. Here the novel turns on its own critique of normalizing forces, linking unconventional gender presentation to psychological defect. Sakamochi is thus subjected to a kind of perverse queering of masculinity against which Shuya, a beautiful young boy who resides squarely within the bounds of a nontraditional but culturally acceptable category of masculinity, represents a comparatively innocuous figure.

The bloodthirsty Kazuo Kiriyama similarly represents a type of masculinity against which Shuya constitutes a preferable alternative. Kazuo rises to the position of gang leader at the behest of his friend Mitsuru, who identifies Kazuo as a quintessential example of traditional masculinity: "There should only be one king, and those who weren't king should serve under him. He reached this conclusion a long time ago. The idea probably came from his favorite shonen manga magazine" (75). Yet beneath Kazuo's stylish exterior, he, too, is affected by psychological perversion, having sustained *in utero* brain damage that has left him a sociopath. Unhampered by emotion and armed with a machine gun, Kazuo is the perfect soldier, but an unlikely hero. As an embodiment of the most extreme possibilities ascribed to Japanese youth, it is only natural that he perish on the island, for his personal victory would entail society's embracement of a kingly monster.

BR's principal female character, Noriko, is likewise a figure whose radical potential is mitigated by her adherence to popularly conceived gender ideals. Noriko does possess a number of remarkable attributes: her superb writing ability (a particularly noteworthy recognition given that men have largely dominated Japan's modern literary canon in terms of acknowledgement, if not in practice); her keen sense of perception; and her level-headedness in times of emotional and physical duress. Yet many of *BR*'s most meaningful depictions of Noriko draw attention away from her intellect and toward those features that serve to identify her with the typical love-struck companions, doting mothers, and naïve young women that permeate traditional narratives.

Perhaps most notably, Noriko shares features with one of manga, anime, and light novels' most stereotypical figures: the girl who has a crush on the hero. You know the type—*Urusei Yatsura*'s Lum Invader, Hinata from *Naruto*, and Orihime from *Bleach*, all of whom, despite their intellectual prowess and/or fighting abilities, serve also to reinforce their male love interests' desirability through their infatuations. Moreover, Noriko's intellect and worldview are limited to geographical and ideological spheres that pose no immediate threat to the status quo. She is talented at writing but has little to offer where warfare is concerned. And while Shuya is enraged by Shogo Kawada's observations of

Greater East Asia's fascist political machine, Noriko clings to her naïve optimism even as her male protectors kill to ensure her survival.

Noriko also exhibits qualities characteristic of a quintessential mother figure. When, for example, Hiroki pays a visit to the clinic in which she, Shuya, and Shogo are hiding out, her domestic side prompts her to remind their guest that the mess is no fault of their own. In another scene, Noriko offers Shuya a comforting hug: "It reminded him of the time his mother hugged him as a child before she died. As he looked at the collar of Noriko's sailor suit, he had a fleeting image of his mother" (122).

A look at two of *BR*'s other female characters further underscores how nicely Noriko aligns with an idealized figuration of femininity. The first is Takako Chigusa, the virginal teen whose excellence in academics and athleticism prompts administrators to overlook her somewhat over-the-top accessorizing, and who murders her attempted rapist, Kazushi. The second is the ruthless Mitsuko Souma, whose hyper-sexualized persona, as we discover, stems from her childhood experience of sexual abuse.

While Takako and Mitsuko would appear to exist at opposite ends of a spectrum, these characters are similar in their expression of perverse sexuality even in the moments leading up to their deaths. Takako is a *bishōjo* (beautiful young girl), an attractive, hardworking, stylish female character type featured across a broad spectrum of Japanese visual and written media. Takako is uninterested in participating in the game, but is nevertheless pulled in when Kazushi insists on taking her virginity before they die. This scene indisputably offers a harsh critique of such attitudes concerning women's bodies. Yet Takako's hesitance to behave as an innocent victim is manifest in the grin that spreads across her face prior to crushing Kazushi's genitals, then finishing him off with an ice pick. Modern Japanese sexologists and mass media outlets have widely attributed criminal acts performed by women to the intrinsic dangers of female sexuality. Takami invokes such perceptions in Takako and Kazushi's scene, wherein Takako's smile comes to signify the sadistic pleasure she derives from inflicting pain on her aggressor. Immediately thereafter her beauty is explicitly linked to her death as Mitsuko arrives on the scene and, confessing her feelings of jealousy toward Takako, murders her.

If Takako is punished for her perverse revenge and unmatched beauty, what do we make of her executioner? Vacillating between angelic and deadly, Mitsuko is a modern day *dokufu*, a "poison woman" whose passion for murder derives from her failure to achieve "normal" psychosexual development. Through recollections of her past, Mitsuko's brutal history of childhood sexual abuse is carefully interwoven with her persona, creating a character who perfectly reflects longstanding medical and cultural discussions of female sexuality as criminal motive. "Maybe I'm a bit of a dyke" (253), she states before her murder of Takako. And whether this is jest, truth, or something in between, that Mitsuko *cannot* survive the game is abundantly clear, for to do so would be to celebrate the triumph of monstrous sexuality over a patriarchal system obsessed with its repression. In Mitsuko's face-off with Kazuo this repression is both physically and symbolically achieved as her beautiful face is riddled with bullets and her eroticized body joins her long-defunct psyche in death.

Takako and Mitsuko exhibit so-called feminine attributes that in Japan have long been considered evidence of the intrinsically disruptive nature of womanhood. Their unchecked beauty and rejection of normative female behavioral codes grant them advantages in the everyday sphere, yet these same advantages lead to downfall in a game designed to re-enforce a nationalist agenda. By contrast, as an "average girl" (11), Noriko's potential for disruption is relatively mild. While she is a far cry from the codified *ryōsai kenbo* (good wife, wise mother) that long dominated Japanese notions of the feminine ideal, her activities as a love-struck companion and motherly nurturer echo historical and contemporary media discourses concerning the predominately passive role of women in social relations.

In its dark yet reservedly optimistic final pages, *BR* celebrates the toppling of rigid political hierarchies as Shuya and Noriko, with the help of self-sacrificing Shogo, defeat the sadistic Sakamochi and escape the island. *BR*'s sustained critique of heavy-handed governmental control mechanisms has garnered the novel, along with its manga and film adaptations, a great deal of much deserved attention. Yet the novel's success relies also on a vast web of other media and social fictions, presenting an image of heroism that at once transgresses negative perceptions of youth culture and remains within the bounds of a gendered moral code. It is in this way that *BR* moves toward advocating a radical restructuring of political hierarchies while ensuring widespread appeal through the preservation of established aesthetic, narrative, and behavioral paradigms. Or, in plain English, how the novel walks the line between political controversy and pop culture convention.

WORK CITED

Takami, Koushun, *Battle Royale: The Novel.* Translated by Yuji Oniki. San Francisco: Haikasoru, 2009.

Girl Power

BY CARRIE CUINN

Battle Royale is often considered a violently misogynistic fantasy, led by strong male characters that propel the story forward,[1] while including "hegemonic stereotypes of girls" who can't help but fall to pieces.[2] Though nominally true, that idea ignores the emotional and even physical strength of the female students. In addition, the insistence on viewing this story as antifeminist highlights the critic's own perspective more than it illuminates the story. Mitsuko Souma, Hirono Shimizu, Yoshimi Yahagi, and Noriko Nakagawa are far more than stereotypes: they stand out as examples of archetypal teenagers: the aspiring femme fatale, the boyish rebel, the teen suicide, and the innocent who must be saved . . . at some point, each uses and loses her power over others and even herself. Though it could be argued that Koushun Takami is suggesting only Noriko deserves to live[3] because she's the final girl (personifying the horror trope of a virginal woman who ends the story by facing down the killer and surviving), the other three girls actually have more agency, and more control, over their ultimate fates. Even so, these four together illustrate how their struggle to have power affects whether they live or die much more than the outside influence of the boys around them.

In the 2012 essay, "*Battle Royale* & Feminist Film Critique," the author argues that the story "depicts young schoolgirls as primarily slow-witted, petty, boy-obsessed, weak, dependent, irrational, and emotional."[4] This essay, posted online by University of Pittsburgh professor Dr. Cathy Hannabach as part of her 2012 Queer & Feminist Film Studies course, is useful because it presents a summary of the arguments against viewing *Battle Royale* in a profeminist light, but it is by no means the only source to critique the material in this way. *Business Insider* said, "Murders break out over simple things—trust issues between friends, girl quarrels over boys (really) or just by accident," as if there is no greater motivation for the characters.[5] The film has been called "politically incorrect exploitation" with "young teenage Asian girls in plaid skirts getting bloodily mowed down."[6] A few perceptive reviewers began to note that "by and large nongenre critics were so shocked—*shocked*—by the premise that the film's nuances went unnoticed,"[7] but the majority continue to focus on the extreme violence, highlighting that "the killing is relentless, shocking, cruel, and bloody"[8] while ignoring the depth of character present in the various schoolgirls.

Takami's work on both the novel and manga explore much more of the girls' lives than can be shown in a movie, but Fukasaku's interpretation makes several changes to the novel's plot that directly increase the amount of power the girls have and take for themselves. Together, they allow for a more positive view of the main female characters. Instead of seeing their "stereotypical predisposition towards animosity with other schoolgirls"[9] as jockeying for position in the eyes of the men around them, why not view the girls as giving more weight to the thoughts, words, and actions of their female classmates than they do those of the boys? In the worlds these girls inhabit, the liminal spaces between home and school, childhood and puberty, dominance and submission, they have formed hierarchies, ranked the male students according to the value gained by possessing one, and already fought amongst themselves for power and security. Mitsuko has explored power from the position of the abuser, while Noriko's innocent sweetness has captivated the boys and even men around her, though her perceptiveness about the greater problems of their student-teacher society leads to a surprising connection with the film-only character of Kitano. Rather than weak, they are wiser than their male counterparts, recognizing how dangerous society truly is before Class 3-B even gets to the island.

> "I just didn't want to be a loser anymore . . ."
> —Mitsuko Souma

Depending on which version of *Battle Royale* you experience, the character of Mitsuko Souma is either the most vicious or the most tragic. In truth, Mitsuko is both. She's the baddest of the bad girls, the one who sells drugs, gets in fights, pimps out her classmates, and murders quite a few of her former pals once they get to the island. We see hints of the former and a whole lot of the latter in the film. She's also been a victim the longest, with a tragic history that is clearly spelled out in the novel and even expanded on in the manga. Moreover, she is betrayed by the feminine ideal—a mother who should protect her but instead treats Mitsuko as a commodity. Mitsuko has finally achieved a small amount of power by the ninth grade, gained by identifying with those who victimized her and becoming the aggressor herself.[10] Without warning, just like when she was beaten as a toddler, sold into sexual abuse as a young girl, or raped as a preteen, selection for the game causes Mitsuko's life to randomly and permanently get even worse through no fault of her own.

Jackson Scarlet of *7x7* says, "*Battle Royale*'s Mitsuko is [third-wave feminism's] unchecked id—raping, robbing and ripping apart boys (and girls) at her slightest whim."[11] Of course she embraces the violence of the game; by killing the other kids, she is limiting the number of people who will have the happy-ever-after she doesn't imagine she can get herself. Unlike those who kill their classmates in the desperate hope they'll live long enough to regret their actions from the safety of their own homes, it's easy to see that all hope was burned out of Mitsuko a long time ago. She has already learned that when bad things happen, no one will come to save her. [12] While the others are forced to fight, she *chooses* instead to take this opportunity to hurt every false friend who ever slighted her. Only by destroying everyone else, Mitsuko believes, can she finally win.

> "Think about what you did!"
> —Hirono Shimizu

Spiky-haired and tough, Hirono Shimizu appears to be an early frontrunner for the final girl, though an injury and subsequent dehydration blinds her to the danger of her last moments. Strangled in the novel and strangled/pushed down into well/drowned while hallucinating in the manga (by Toshinori Oda, both times), Hirono is doomed to die like most of the other students, but in the film she's shot by Mitsuko instead. Hirono's life is taken by another *girl,* instead of her being killed at the hands of a boy. Hirono's dialogue is limited but almost entirely consists of valid accusations. She points out that Mitsuko has lied, sold her friends into prostitution, and betrayed the people who trusted her, and in this way, she has become the voice of Mitsuko's self-hating anger. Hirono's words hold up a mirror that reflects not Mitsuko as she wants to see herself, confident and worthy of respect, but the Mitsuko who has become the worst aspects of her mother's neglect. Hirono's strength in this moment not only drives her former friend to murder, but it also depicts the reason Hirono is on her own when most of the other girls have found friends to partner up with. In the novel she can be seen lacking the filters necessary to play nice with her classmates, sneering instead at the supposed weakness that friendship implies. She searched for a friend with a strong personality because she needed to feel she didn't simply fall in with a crowd. She wanted to be chosen, special, and this shared need—along with their fierce spirits—united the two girls as allies long before the game began.

If there is any weakness at all in these characters, it is only this: Mitsuko-the-child couldn't find the power to confront her own mother the way Hirono stands up to her in the moments before her death. If she had, Mitsuko might have kept her strength of personality while escaping the cycle of victim-turned-abuser, and though their fate would inevitably bring them to the island, perhaps neither girl would have died friendless.

" . . "

—Yoshimi Yahagi

What do you do when you know for a fact you'll die a horrible death in less than seventy-two hours? If you don't have a victim's need for vengeance, a sociopath's desire to revel in the pain of others, or the ability to convince yourself that your life is more important than everyone else's, you can either wait for someone to kill you, or you can take back the power to die on your own terms. Yoshimi, who doesn't have a single line of dialogue in the film, chooses to hang herself alongside her boyfriend, Yoji. She doesn't die alone, she isn't betrayed by her friends, and she doesn't have to wonder in her final moments if she is loved. In the real world, a child's suicide is tragic, and Yoshimi's end is certainly that, but in the horrible context of the game, it is also the strongest decision she could have made.

In the novel, Yoshimi is portrayed as a baby-faced urban girl who does regrettable things because she feels misunderstood and unwanted by her parents. She lets Mitsuko manipulate her because she's looking for a way to fill the void in her chest, but Mitsuko's friendship and the thrill of life on the edge can't compare to her relationship with Yoji, who encourages her to be a better person. It's this relationship that distracts the couple from the threat around them; they're killed by Mitsuko on the first day of battle. The manga provides a little more background, painting Yoshimi as fragile, obsessive, and on the verge of mental collapse. (Who could forget her trying to put Yoji's spilt brains back into his head, so he wouldn't make a mess?) The film's truncated image of this girl takes away those flaws and allows her to be young. She makes mistakes, falls in love, feels regret, and so can be seen as a Juliet figure whose final act puts her out of the reach of everyone who would hurt her, ever again.

> "Before this, I always just thought of myself as
> normal. I'd have a normal marriage, age normally,
> just like my mom . . . but when this game started,
> I realized—it's just that I was sheltered."
> —Noriko Nakagawa

That Noriko comes to understand her role as the innocent doesn't mean she breaks free of it. She's the final girl, but she survives the majority of the story by becoming so sick that she needs to be cared for by others, rather than through any action of her own. Her last meeting with Kitano in the film version isn't the confrontation you'd expect from the horror trope, and her escape from the island seems to be allowed rather than won. She could have easily ended up like Hirono—confused, helpless, unable to defend herself—if she wasn't protected by the male heroes, who need to see her as a stand-in for someone else rather than valuing her (at least initially) for herself.

Though *io9* criticized the affection the other characters have for Noriko as unrealistic, saying it was difficult to become emotionally invested in the story "since everyone is so ridiculously in love with" her,[13] the print versions of *Battle Royale* offer a more developed explanation. To Shuya Nanahara, she's a reminder of his dead best friend, who had a crush on her. Shuya needs to protect her the way he believes Nobu Yoshitoki would have, and Noriko accepts his help without argument. To Shogo Kawada, Noriko is a stand-in for his dead girlfriend, Keiko, whom he lost in a previous iteration of the game. Shogo saves Noriko and Shuya to prove to himself that a young couple in love can survive the evil thrust on them by a heartless government—even though he has no reason to believe they really love each other. He needs to see himself in them, and they need to survive, so Noriko complies. Yet, her naïve persona is merely the shell of a girl who is neither as submissive nor as perfect as she appears.

Several moments in the story highlight this dichotomy. In the film, she is "portrayed as a deity by Kitano, featuring in a painting with a halo surrounding her head while her fellow peers lie dead beside her,"[14] but when he chants, "Noriko, you can do it. Noriko, you can do it!" he's actually encouraging her to shoot him so he can die at her hand. When the fever from her injury causes her to dream, she imagines a beautiful stroll by the river with her teacher, but calmly admits that after he was stabbed, she took home the bloody knife as a memento of the incident. And though she's been dismissed as the "useless" one for much of the story, when Kawada is critically injured and Shuya collapses in grief, waiting to die, it's Noriko who shoots Kiriyama and possibly kills him. In the manga, she contacts her mother after she's fled the island, but when she's faced with the choice of returning to Japan as a criminal or disappointing her mother, she breaks with the traditional ideal of the dutiful daughter and accepts that to live she'll have to be a failure in her family's eyes. Noriko's real power may be her ability to let people around her decide who she is at that moment, but this apparent helplessness actually puts her in a position to save herself in the end.

It's fair to say that the types of girl power exhibited in *Battle Royale* might not be as obvious to Western viewers, who often have to discard their cultural expectations when experiencing entertainment from Japan in order to properly appreciate the works. "Girls in Japan don't use words like feminist or Riot Grrl, etc," said Petty Booka in 2004. "There are not even any Japanese words that equal these ideas."[15] It is especially important to note that where "Western stories stress the search for perfection by eliminating or destroying any sort of imperfection, Japanese stories stress the completeness or wholeness accomplished by accepting everything in life, including any imperfections that may exist."[16] The children of Class 3-B are damaged by their society, their families, sexual abuse, drug use, and even their class-mates, before they have a chance to grow up. Finally, fatally, they are thrown into an impossible situation and told to become monsters for a chance to survive. That these girls—in fact, all of the schoolgirls in the story—are broken to begin with does not make them any less powerful. Though certainly terrified, the girls are less surprised at the necessary violence than the boys because they've already seen the world darkly, and those with the most horrible pasts are better equipped to decide on their next action.

Yet Western audiences are given enough material, in the form of a novel, manga series, and film, to understand that Mitsuko Souma, Hirono Shimizu, Yoshimi Yahagi, and even Noriko Nakagawa make choices that directly inform their fates. Their power isn't a gift from the males around them; Mitsuko kills more than one boy by luring him close with her flirtatious advances, while Shuya repeatedly puts him-self into harm's way to get Noriko what she needs because she wants him to. By ignoring that, the viewer is dismissing the girls' free will and their circumstances. Anyone engaging with the material—outside of the plot—can choose to interpret the female characters as less than they are written, but on paper and on-screen, the girls of Class 3-B are clever, resilient, independent, loving, insightful, maternal, vindictive, strong, and terrifying, when they choose to be. What could be more powerful than that?

ENDNOTES

1 D.M. Haight, *KineCritical,* February 2013. http://kinecritical.blogspot.com/2013/02/lessons-taught-battle-royale.html

2 *"Battle Royale* & Feminist Film Critique," posted online by Dr. Cathy Hannabach, April 19, 2012. http://pittqueerfemfilm.wordpress.com/2012/04/19/battle-royale-feminist-film-critique/

3 Samara L. Allsop, *"Battle Royale*—Challenging global stereotypes within the constructs of a contemporary Japanese slasher film," *Film Journal,* Issue 7, 2002. http://www.thefilmjournal.com/issue7/battleroyale.html

4 *"Battle Royale* & Feminist Film Critique," posted online by Dr. Cathy Hannabach.

5 Kirsten Acuna, *Business Insider,* April 3, 2012. http://www.businessinsider.com/the-hunger-games-is-not-battle-royale-despite-many-similarities-2012-4?op=1

6 *Joblo.* http://www.joblo.com/horror-movies/reviews/battle-royale

7 Maitland McDonagh, *Film Journal International,* May 25, 2012. http://www.filmjournal.com/filmjournal/content_display/reviews/specialty-releases/e3ie47a970ce53a118571851be800cb7637

8 Joshua Rothman, *New Yorker,* April 3, 2012. http://www.newyorker.com/online/blogs/culture/2012/04/the-real-hunger-games-battle-royale.html

9 *"Battle Royale* & Feminist Film Critique," posted online by Dr. Cathy Hannabach.

10 Anna Freud, *The Ego and the Mechanisms of Defence,* Karnac Books, 1992.

11 Jackson Scarlett, *7x7 SF,* April 13, 2012. http://www.7x7.com/arts-culture/7-reasons-skip-hunger-games-and-see-battle-royale-tonight

12 Anthony Antoniou, "Batoru Rowairu / Battle Royale," *The Cinema of Japan and Korea,* ed. Justin Bowyer, Wallflower Press, 2004, 225..

13 Meridith Woerner, *iO9,* February 24, 2012. http://io9.com/5888124/did-the-hunger-games-really-rip-off-battle-royale

14 Allsop, *"Battle Royale*—Challenging global stereotypes."

15 Xenia Shin, "Japanese Girl Power—Even If There Isn't a Word for It," UCLA International Institute, March 19, 2004. http://www.international.ucla.edu/article.asp?parentid=9066

16 David Endresak, "Girl Power: Feminine Motifs in Japanese Popular Culture," Eastern Michigan University, 2006. http://commons.emich.edu/cgi/viewcontent.cgi?article=1321&context=honors

Over the Top, or Over the Top Rope? *Battle Royale* and Japan's Love of Professional Wrestling

BY JASON S. RIDLER

Without professional wrestling, there is no *Battle Royale*.

In the introduction to the novel, author Koushun Takami gives us a quick and dirty description of what, indeed, a battle royale is: a special wrestling match where many wrestlers, usually twenty, start in the ring together. When the bell rings, hell breaks loose. Every wrestler tries to throw the others over the top rope and have their opponent's feet touch the floor below. The last wrestler left in the ring is the winner.

Why is such an introduction necessary? I mean, could you imagine a best-selling book with a baseball motif requiring an introductory chapter called "An Introduction to the Grand Slam"? Of course not. So why is such a hook needed with *Battle Royale*?

Because even in an age where World Wrestling Entertainment (WWE) is a global phenomenon and Hulk Hogan, Stone Cold Steve Austin, and the Rock are part of pop culture writ large, pro wrestling lurks in the shadows of the literary world. Even with best-selling memoirs from wrestlers like Chris Jericho and Mick Foley (who has, like Winston Churchill, published three volumes of memoir), the literati maintain that pro wrestling is for barbarians who would probably rip a book in half or set it on fire as soon as read it.

Public intellectual Christopher Hedges, who had the decency to watch wrestling matches before commenting on them, sees the lurid world of pro wrestling as a dark mirror of the economic collapse in the US, the storylines playing out as psychodramas for those in hard times.

> They are public expressions of pain and a fervent longing for revenge. The lurid and detailed sagas behind each bout, rather than the wrestling matches themselves, are what drive crowds to a frenzy. These ritualized battles give those packed in the arenas a temporary, heady release from mundane lives. The burden of real problems is transformed into fodder for a high-energy panto-mime. . . . For most, it is only in the illusion of the ring that they are able to rise above their small stations in life and engage in a heroic battle to fight back. As the wrestlers appear and strut down the aisle, the crowd, mostly young, working-class males, knows by heart the long list of vendettas and betrayals being carried into the ring. . . . The narratives of emotional wreckage reflected in the wrestlers' stage biographies mirror the emotional wreckage of the fans. This is the deep appeal of professional wrestling.[1]

And why does it work? Because "we ask to be fooled. We happily pay for the chance to suspend reality. The wrestlers, like all celebrities, become our vicarious selves."[2]

Sounds a lot like *Battle Royale,* doesn't it?

Modern pro wrestling was born in the 1920s when the slow pace of authentically competitive grappling matches began to bore audiences. Choreographed exhibitions, predetermined winners, and larger-than-life characters and "gimmicks" quickly supplanted the actual sport. Pro wrestling then became an art form and, ultimately, transformed into a big money-maker. Many nations have taken the American form, mixed it with their own theatrics and historical combat arts, and turned pro wrestling into a cultural industry with national heroes, villains, storylines, and grudges that thrill millions. While Canada, Great Britain, and Mexico all boast strong wrestling industries, few places embraced pro wrestling like postwar Japan. In the aftermath of the Second World War, Japanese wrestlers became cultural icons and pop stars to a generation living in the wake of defeat and demilitarization. From these ashes, the need for heroes was great, and even as the generations rolled on, pro wrestling was forever a part of Japan's pop culture landscape.[3]

Including, of course, *Battle Royale.* The style and structure of a pro wrestling battle royale—of gang warfare in an isolated space, of short-term alliances that end in betrayal, of hidden weapons and cheats, of a game rigged to have one victor and many bodies in an anything-goes world—have a direct structural parallel to the novel that shares its name. Much of the intrigue of the novel *Battle Royale* comes from how the children are killed or how they choose to die. Each weapon, style, and moment is a unique signature. The kids start out in school uniforms, and what defines them most are their relationships to each other and the way they finally die. In wrestling, pro wrestlers do everything they can to make themselves distinct and not look like everyone else—a challenge given near-identical bodybuilder physiques. This ranges from costumes to physical defects or anomalies, and other gimmicks. They also all have a signature fighting style and a "finishing move" that allows them to beat their opponents. The finisher, much like the weapons and methods of death in *Battle Royale,* defines the person who uses it. A giant uses some devastating power move; an intelligent villain employs a cruel submission hold; a happy-go-lucky hero climbs to the top turnbuckle and flies across the ring to pin his opponent.

If pro wrestling wasn't integral to the novel's structure, if any other sport could fit Takami's tastes, you'd have a story about a bunch of kids who form teams with balls or bats and kill other teams, and the novel would be called *Slam Dunk* or *Hat-Trick* or *Touchdown.* And it would be awful. The underlying ethos of *Battle Royale* is a direct reflection of Japan's long-held traditions, fascinations, and obsession with professional wrestling. And it's an influence that almost no one talks about. We read about George Orwell's *Nineteen Eighty-Four,* Stephen King's *The Long Walk* or his short story "Running Man," or the Japanese television show *Kinpachi Sensei,* or how *The Hunger Games* aped its structure and world-building. But even when the title of the book references one of the most identifiable matches in pro wrestling, there is nary a peep.

Takami says that when the idea for the novel came to him, he was "something of a pro wrestling fan, and even though I had seen any number of 'battle royal'–style matches (or possibly because I had seen so many), I didn't understand the true meaning of the rule, 'Anyone can face off against anyone else.'"[4] So he played around with the idea of kids helping each other as they kill each other in a dystopian world where a pro wrestling game is made real, lethal, and final. The result? A pop culture masterpiece!

THE AUTHOR AND HIS BRAWNY MUSE

Takami was raised on both American and Japanese varieties of pro wrestling in the 1980s and 1990s, when the then-World Wrestling Federation (now WWE) became an international sensation. But of the American wrestlers of the era, Takami liked the rougher, rowdier characters who often performed in Japan. "I'm sure some of you know who Stan Hansen is," he noted in the afterword to the 2009 US edition. How adorable that he thinks we all know the former AWA champ, a huge, brawny cowboy who chewed tobacco in the ring and was master of both the heart punch and lariat! "[W]hen he entered the ring in All Japan Pro-Wrestling, what a shock it was! All sorts of foreign wrestlers have done it since then, but watching him devastate one Japanese wrestler after another—even my idol, Asura Hara—with his lariat was really the biggest shock. (Had I seen the Road Warriors before Hansen, my reaction may have been different.) On top of that, he had a rugged, Western appearance that remained somehow charming, no matter how tough his performance in the ring."[5]

Takami also enjoyed the high-flying Dynamite Kid and his powerhouse cousin Davey Boy Smith—known together as the British

Bulldogs—and of course Japanese legends like Asura Hara, Giant Baba, and Jumbo Tsuruta from All Japan Wrestling, one of the two major promotions in the country. (The other is New Japan, associated with Antonio Inoki.) "I think the appeal of pro wrestling can be summed up, as Giant Baba once said, as 'big, strong men charging at each other,'" Takami argues. "Tsuruta had a substantially large build for a Japanese man. As an amateur wrestler, he competed in the Olympics, and his execution of Lou Thesz's back drop was beautiful. (He came down with hepatitis and died due to complications in transplant surgery.) He was typically calm, and his face was free of maliciousness even inside the ring." [6]

The architecture of these matches that Takami loved, however, lay in the ashes of Imperial Japan's defeat in 1945. The nation's psyche was shattered. Giant Americans walked around the "occupied" home islands as if they owned the joint. Surrounded by the aftermath of war and atomic destruction, thousands of Japanese men and women found solace, and inspiration, not in the real violence of the past two decades, but in a mirage of violence that was in fact tightly scripted cooperation.

POST-ATOMIC WRESTLING

Like the US, Mexico, Germany, and Canada, Japan developed a unique brand of pro wrestling that captivated generations after the Second World War. Indeed, their greatest pro wrestling hero, Rikidōzan, was as much a pop culture icon as El Santo or Hulk Hogan, in part because he emerged from the wreckage of Japan's defeat in 1945. What thousands and then millions found in Rikidōzan was a figure of hope, of power, of manliness that could symbolically defeat all that threatened Japan by performing in the ring. He was an icon, especially when he fought American wrestlers: one man against the odds, standing alone, fighting his own way. Just like Shuya in *Battle Royale,* teaming with like-minded folks but often standing apart from the crowd for his nonviolent desires.

But as with any wrestling tale, there's a twist. Unlike Shuya, our hero wasn't really Japanese but Korean. And thus, both are outcasts from the worlds they inhabit.

Japan's immediate recovery from the Second World War was brutal. The militant culture of the Imperial Japanese government, filled as it was with ardent nationalism, racial hierarchies, and brutal occupation policies, had been beaten by Western powers, including the use of two atomic weapons. In the wake of this defeat, Western influences wrestled with old traditions as Japan recovered and recreated its national identity, and generational divides grew between the older generation and those raised in the aftermath. [7]

Rikidōzan symbolized Japanese honor and strength and the ability to defeat any and all who challenged him. During *The Mitsubishi Fightman Hour,* fans would watch as Rikidōzan vanquished legions of foes. But of all the many foes Rikidōzan would face, none were more dastardly than Americans. US wrestlers began coming to Japan during the occupation period, and they were almost always cast as villains when touring Japan: they cheated, they brawled, they used foreign objects including brass knuckles, and, always, they were bullies. Crowds abhorred and despised these incarnations of American dominance in the wake of the Second World War. And that hate was pure "heat" in wrestling terms: it sold tickets. Because almost every wrestling fan in Japan wanted to see the American foe vanquished. And the man who accomplished this task for Japan was Rikidōzan.

And he was Korean.

Born in 1924, during Imperial Japan's occupation of Korea, Kim Sin-rak trained as a sumo wrestler where, according to one biopic, his Korean heritage made him an outcast and bottom feeder. [8] He even changed his name to Rikidōzan and claimed to be from the atomically devastated Nagasaki. Never accepted into the "real" world of sports, Rikidōzan joined Japan's emerging pro wrestling field in 1951, where his natural charisma and athleticism soon made him a star. But what made him an icon was how he fought his matches.

Like all babyfaces (heroes) of this era of wrestling, Rikidōzan was held up as a model of noble virtue. Babyfaces played by the rules. They were fair. They were honorable. All of which made them saps for villains who attacked them from behind before the match officially started—a narrative routine known for years in the US as a "Pearl Harbor Job." Rikidōzan would often take serious beatings from cheating, thuggish Americans, many of whom were soldiers and Marines in the occupation force who did wrestling for kicks and fast cash. But, when all was dark, and hope seemed to vanish, Rikidōzan would make an explosive comeback. Hard openhanded slaps, Sumo style, would thrash the barrel chests and necks of the Americans, who could not stand the assault. They'd be knocked over by his own vicious shoulder block, judo flips, as well as popular wrestling staples like hammerlocks, headlocks, and body slams.

But his overhand chops cut men down to kindling for the 1-2-3.

And the reverberations of his matches were an economic boom! According to Robert Whiting, the chief wrestling show, *The Mitsubishi Fightman Hour,* was like a steroid shot into the Japanese electronics industry. The show was so popular that "sales of TV sets had skyrocketed from the 1954 plateau of 17,000 to more than 4,500,000 by 1959. One of [Rikidōzan's] matches—a draw with NWA champion Lou Thesz before 27,000 fans at Tokyo's outdoor Korakuen Stadium in 1956—had attracted the largest crowd ever to watch a wrestling event in Japan and had earned a Japanese Nielsen rating of 87 percent, a domestic record that would be surpassed only by the carriage-drawn wedding procession of the Crown Prince and Princess through the heart of Tokyo."[9]

Rikidōzan became an inspirational folk hero, part of pop culture and modern Japanese mythology, in the same way El Santo would become such in Mexico about the same time. His style of matches, of being brutalized and making a Herculean comeback, were the staple of his American counterpart in the 1980s, Hulk Hogan.

Battle Royale, however, champions as well as inverts the Rikidōzan myth, as well as explores the grotesqueries of violent entertainment. Our hero, Shuya Nanahara, almost a real babyface, is much like

Rikidōzan. He is an unwanted orphan who must make his own way against the momentum of history. Like Rikidōzan, Shuya is a charismatic, self-described "rock star," but one who doesn't want to follow the rules, which only serve the vicious. His moral code, however, of doing what's right, of protecting his best friend's crush, Noriko, after his friend is killed, of trying everything he can to escape and not become a pawn of the game, are all heroic notions. But Shuya is a distorted image of Rikidōzan in critical aspects: nonviolence, loving of American rebel culture like rock and roll and Bruce Springsteen, and seeking to escape the nightmare dystopia of the Republic of Greater East Asia and find freedom in the US. The odds are the same, the comebacks are similar—only the target of villainy changes. The final confrontation with the evil supervisor Kinpatsu Sakamochi, though, plays out in classic Rikidōzan style. Pushed to the brink, Shogo stabs Sakamochi in the neck with a "foreign object," in this case, a pencil. One can almost hear the echoes of wrestler Classy Freddy Blassie's quip about "pencil-neck geeks" being played out.

Rikidōzan, sadly, did not reach his dream shores like Shuya but became a victim of his own excesses. A powerful entertainment guru even after he stopped wrestling, Rikidōzan ran afoul of the yakuza. In a moment that is still hazy and controversial, Rikidōzan, drunk and boisterous, disrespected a junior member of the yakuza at a nightclub. He was later stabbed with a urine-soaked blade and died shortly after of peritonitis in December 1963.

From the morality play Rikidōzan constructed, the world of pro wrestling continued to grow in Japan into the even more flamboyant styles of the 1980s that Takami loved. It was an era of acrobats and strongmen and matches that still looks fresh, deadly, and exciting today. Wrestlers such as Tiger Mask or the Dynamite Kid fought against each other in explosive confrontations that bordered on the superhuman. Both had serious countenances until the match started, at which point all hell broke loose.

Including when friends turned on each other.

Perhaps the most constant saga in pro wrestling is the "double cross." Time and time again, "babyfaces" gather allies to fight cadres of "heels" who pack together to commit mayhem: the Legion of Doom, the Freebirds, the Four Horseman and the New World Order are only some of the gangs that run roughshod over individual wrestlers, often led by managers who are the only ones who can control the wild antics of their charges. But occasionally, a wrestler goes rogue. In *Battle Royale,* the manager and mad wrestler scenario is played out by Mitsuru and Kazuo. Before the games commence, Mitsuru is the leader of a small gang of kids. When a rival gang attacks him, the sociopathic killing machine Kazuo destroys the attackers more for kicks than to help. With Mitsuru's aid, "the king" of combat Kazuo and "his loyal advisor" Mitsuru initially team up against the other students. But when Mitsuru sees the dead-eyed Kazuo casually kill the rest of the gang with no provocation, the chains are off the beast and Mitsuru is killed by a hail of bullets from Kazuo. [10]

In 1986, Hulk Hogan enlisted the aid of a one-time adversary, Paul "Mr. Wonderful" Orndorff. Over time, their friendship became mired with jealousy, and after saving Hogan from a brutal beating, Orndorff raised Hogan's hand in victory . . . only to clothesline him to the ground and start a feud that would draw big money at the aptly named Big Event at Toronto's CNE stadium. In *Battle Royale,* double crosses, "heel" turns for babyfaces, and backstabs are just as common. In fact, they are the core of the drama, as the reader waits to see who will turn on who and whether friendship can survive a game designed to destroy it. Teams are made, friendships forged, and double crosses abound. Poisoned food backfires on Yuko Sakaki, one of the so-called neutrals, when an attempt to kill Shuya ends up killing Yuka Nakagawa and starts a mini battle royale where her treachery leads to carnage.

In *Battle Royale,* the lives of the young are dismissed and used as mere props for propaganda, human material to feed the needs of the totalitarian state. They have no humanity to the system that employs them, beyond the function of the game. It is a very cold calculus, to be sure. And it also reflects a trend in professional wrestling that grows every year.

Modern wrestlers die young. Drugs, insane work schedules, alcohol, and a rock-and-roll lifestyle, plied to limited chance for sustainable success, have bred a culture of lives half lived. Many wrestlers who came of age when pro wrestling popped in the 1980s are dead. Even younger ones are ending up with heart attacks, car crashes, or grisly deaths as their epitaphs before they push fifty, let alone sixty. People talk of surviving pro wrestling like surviving the island in *Battle Royale*. It's not a career, it's a mortal gamble.

Takami knew this truth all too well. Childhood heroes like Hawk of the Road Warriors/Legion of Doom and Davey Boy Smith of the British Bulldogs, both muscle-bound giants capable of amazing feats in the ring, abused drugs so much that they either wore out their internal organs or succumbed to lethal addictions. Hawk died at forty-six. Smith at thirty-nine. Takami recalls that both Road Warrior Hawk and Davey Boy Smith "seemed wrapped in armor made of muscle, but I think their sudden and premature deaths . . . were related to that very muscle." In *Battle Royale,* being young and innocent cannot save you from the murderous world. In pro wrestling, being a giant can be a death warrant. Both are compelling points, if tragic.

"As a pro wrestling fan," Takami said, "I will say up front they didn't need to go that far for us, but they did, and in so doing, they were an inspiration to us in our youth. For that I thank them from the bottom of my heart . . . In Japan Shinya Hashimoto left us, also at a young age. I hope all three are in a better place."[11]

Even now, with so many wrestlers not making it to fifty, *Battle Royale*'s love affair with young people killing themselves in a blood sport is prescient. The only ones who get out alive are the ones who do not succumb in totality to the brutal conditions they are forced into. They maintain their sense of self and humanity. They do not let their egos grow into the superhuman characters they portray, thinking themselves invulnerable to drugs, injuries, or a yakuza's blade. The deaths of Hawk, Davey Boy Smith, and Rikidōzan, to name only three, are far more sad and brutal than those of the young people in *Battle Royale*. Because they were real, even if wrestling, like the novel, is fiction.

ENDNOTES

1 Chris Hedges, *Empire of Illusion: The End of Literacy and the Triumph of Spectacle* (New York: Nation Books, 2009), 5.

2 Hedges, *Empire of Illusion,* 6.

3 Robert Whiting, *Tokyo Underground: The Fast Times and Hard Life of an American Gangster in Japan* (New York: Vintage, 2000), 49–56.

4 Koushun Takami, Afterword, *Battle Royale: The Novel,* trans. Yuji Oniki (San Francisco: Haikasoru, 2009), 593.

5 Takami, Afterword, *Battle Royale,* 599.

6 Takami, Afterword, *Battle Royale,* 599.

7 In Kazuo Ishiguro's *Artist of the Floating World,* this challenge between generations is explored through a family struggling with the pre-war jingoism that infects one father's life, art, and psychology, and the friction it creates with his family in the wake of Hiroshima and Nagasaki.

8 Hae-sung Song (dir.), *Rikidozan: A Hero Extraordinary* (2004).

9 Whiting, *Tokyo Underground,* 79.

10 Takami, *Battle Royale,* 70–83.

11 Takami, Afterword, *Battle Royale,* 598–599.

Battle Royale
Generational Warfare

BY KOSTAS PARADIAS

Battle Royale requires no introduction. A work of horror with unrivaled shock value, a story that revolves around a blood sport—supposedly—set up by a dystopian dictatorship that pits junior high school children against one another under the guise of a government-sanctioned purge.

But for all its blood, gore, and teenage terror, *Battle Royale* hides another, subtler theme that is at first obscured to the reader (or viewer), becoming apparent upon closer scrutiny. In the movie adaptation, it is made clearer thanks to the playful (and darkly funny) presentation by the announcer, played by Yūko Miyamura.

Battle Royale is not a governmental extermination program set up by uncaring, immoral G-men and stone-faced bureaucrats; instead, it is—explicitly in the manga—a reality show of sorts. It has prizes. It carries severe penalties for cheating contestants. And it is watched by millions. The premise alone guarantees that such an event wouldn't stand unless it had an audience that would tolerate such cruelty.

Within this context, a new question rises concerning *Battle Royale*'s setting and execution, as well as the specifics of its narrative: if this is not the product of shadowy forces, set up by a shadowy dictatorship, if this is actually some sort of franchise, a national pastime, then where does the consumer demand that supports it come from?

To understand, we need to look into the life of *Battle Royale* author Koushun Takami, as well as into the social situation in Japan in the years of his youth until the late nineties, when the novel *Battle Royale* was written.

JAPAN'S GROWTH AND THE ADVENT OF THE *BOSOZOKU*

Author Koushun Takami was born on January 10, 1969, and lived his formative years during the exponential growth of the Japanese economy, which lasted from 1952 to the 1990s. After a period of social disharmony and near economic collapse following World War II, Japan had managed—through careful investments and a number of bold political and economic maneuvers—to achieve what was then called the Japanese postwar economic miracle. Japan had risen from its ashes and become one of the fastest developing nations worldwide, its crime rate reaching a low dubbed "almost paradoxical"[1] by criminologists of that time, attributed by sociologists to the country's cultural structure and tradition. The main point of sociological focus was the Japanese ideal of "group consciousness,"[2] which was the focus of traditional Japanese society: the ideal of the group caring for the individuals comprising it, the individuals themselves caring for the group in turn. Harmony within the group, a perfect example of applied Confucianism ideology.

But even in this time of prosperity, juvenile crime still troubled Japanese society. Its rate or frequency may not have been as high as in the rest of the world; however, a new unforeseen factor, the *bosozoku* (the Japanese equivalent of biker gangs) became the focus of the debate on crime and a very clear indication of social unrest. Led by members of the lowest rungs of the yakuza and originating from descendants of the *burakumin* caste—a class of traditional Japanese society consisting of those performing menial or unclean labor, such as undertakers, tanners, or coal miners—these teenagers found themselves oppressed by law and social prejudice.[3]

Denied employment and perhaps even a future, they evolved into groups of knife-wielding thugs that mostly perpetrated small-time heists or muggings, the scope of their influence considered too petty for organized crime standards. It wasn't until 1990, when crime in Japan skyrocketed,[4] that these biker gangs suddenly ceased to be a nuisance to their elders and transmuted into poster children for criminal activity.

But what were the bosozoku exactly? Today, they are little more than a subcultural Japanese oddity: the "juvenile" gangs are now mostly comprised of adults well above the age of twenty who focus more on modifying their motorcycles according to their gang's outrageous style than engaging in illegal activities.[5] But that was not always the case.

The term *bosozoku* itself—coined in the 1960s—translates to "speed tribes." These "speed tribes"[6] chose for themselves the most flamboyant, over-the-top names, such as "Death Squad" and "Black Emperor," and their sole purpose was to achieve the maximum possible speed in any given circumstance and to make as much noise as possible in a display of horsepower. Their signature dress, colored jumpsuits decorated with obscure Chinese characters, symbolic of the roots of some of their members—their parents descendants of Korean or Chinese refugees—made the speed tribes iconic. These jumpsuits were similar to those of manual laborers, an obvious tribute to the subculture's class basis. They were called *tokko-fuku,* named after the uniform of the kamikaze pilots in World War II. On the road, the bosozoku are known to engage in acrobatics and were famous for harassing drivers on highways as a source of cheap thrills. It is a culture characterized by over-the-top displays and mostly caters to attention-seekers or andrenaline addicts. It was a culture of bike enthusiasts, with members ranging from fifteen to eighteen years old, with every member quitting on their twentieth birthday.[7] This initial description of the bosozoku's outrageous style does little in the way of presenting them as the ferocious delinquents everyone would like to think they were. In fact, from the 1960s (with the boom of the Japanese automotive industry) until the end of the 1980s, the bosozoku's primary purpose was mostly exhibitionist, with very few (and in fact, extreme) instances of actual recorded criminal activity.

During the 1990s, the bosozoku look also included *hachimaki* headbands, to help maintain their signature outrageous rockabilly coiffure, a hairstyle that was passed on to the bosozoku by the yakuza, following their introduction into organized crime.

Thus, the bosozoku made their way into Japanese pop culture and became a staple of youth delinquency. Since then, popular culture has made the bosozoku both villains and heroes in numerous manga and televised dramas, presenting their outbursts of violence as untempered and shortsighted until the mid-nineties, when they were finally inducted into the yakuza. The main character of the *Battle Royale* manga adaptation, Shuya Nanahara, sports a haircut much like that (and is dubbed 'Elvis' by Mr. Kamon, in an obvious nod to the fad).

Japan was entering a period in its modern history that would become known as the Lost Decade (1991–2001), when the exponential economic growth of Japan suddenly ceased and its bubble simply burst. The manufacturing firms that were maintaining Japan's economy fell apart, and the banks found themselves going bankrupt, as enterprises could no longer afford to service the loans that were used to found them. Unemployment rates soared, and an alarming percentage of the many unemployed youths turned to crime.

When the Japanese economy came tumbling down, the bosozoku (already existing in the fringes of society) found themselves in danger of losing their own culture as well. The household problems that emerged as a result of the economic collapse—heated domestic disputes, absent fathers, a general feeling of nationwide depression, as is appropriate to times of financial hardship—only helped to spur those youths into openly violent activities. The children without a future found themselves hitting the road as often as they could, looking for ways to vent their frustration. This, however, was not an adequate reason to explain the sudden boom in bosozoku numbers, maintaining a steady forty thousand total members for the duration of the nineties. It was, in fact, the result of the creation of a counter-school culture.[8] As children of the working class, these youths were very much aware that their parents could not afford the tutors and the high fees required to ensure enrollment in prestigious high schools, which would in turn provide them with a better education and better career opportunities. Painfully aware of their bleak futures, these teenagers instead lashed out against their schools and teachers and created their own sets of rules that rejected the expectations of a society obsessed with middle-class values.

The first widespread instances of organized bosozoku activites were called *oyaji-gari,* or "dad-hunts." These involved baiting salary-men over the age of forty with attractive girls to lead them into an isolated place and then assault them—in some cases, outright killing them—to steal their money. Other times, these hunts would target middle-aged housewives or even students on their way home from school or on field trips, though the latter were more for the sake of fun rather than profit.

Other bosozoku gangs focused on muggings and organized them-selves by meeting on Saturdays, performing over a hundred street muggings a week in order to reach one-hundred-thousand-yen goals. These gangs mostly consisted of middle and high school students, who were heavily indebted to local crime bosses that swiped most of their take.

The bosozoku gangs with the youngest members (in some cases, as young as ten years old) would simply go on sprees, targeting the homeless at night and beating them or killing them outright, without any intention of monetary gain. They called it "killing time," and when interrogated by the police, they explained that to them, this was a means of "relieving stress."

In his book *Speed Tribes: Days and Nights with Japan's Next Generation,* Karl Taro Greenfeld presents the lower-class origin of bosozoku society: they were the children of industrial workers, laborers, and workers who built the country and paved the roads the bosozoku rode on, who paved with their hard work a life of plenty for the lucky few but found their own children excluded from this lavish, opulent lifestyle.[9] While the consumers stampeded for a chance to get their hands on luxury goods from Tiffany's, the bosozoku instead focused on investing every last yen they made into illegally modifying their vehicles with loud exhaust pipes and in maintaining their outrageous appearances. When that all fell apart in the Lost Decade, they found their identities threatened and opted for another solution.

But what was the reason for this sudden shift to openly antisocial, criminal behavior? The answer is upward mobility.[10] For the children of the burakumin, their only choice was a chance at adoption by the yakuza. As the possibility of finding a better life for themselves by following the straight and narrow seemed very slim indeed, they turned their attention to drawing the eye of the organized crime families, hoping that perhaps from there they could find a successful criminal patron to provide for them. In this manner, they appear very much like the children of poor American families turning to the Mafia for help: a way out of the gutter into perhaps a gilded one, where they could look up at high society and pretend like it was all worth it.

According to National Police Agency reports, in 1995, "a remarkable increase in the number of juveniles taken into custody by police for using amphetamines has been observed since the second half of last year" (Asahi News Service, September 9, 1996). By 1996, an alarming increase of larcenies and crimes classified as "violent offenses" was noticed through the examination of official police reports.[11] Furthermore, the number of such offenses targeting older people past the age of fifty had increased, indicating "drastic changes in the environment which surrounds elderly people."[12] Media at the time made exaggerated, statistically uncorroborated reports of spectacular murders perpetrated by teenagers. But even in the face of such frenzy, the rate of homicide remained at an all-time high.

It did not help that at the time the estimated number of bosozoku gangs was over a thousand. Now integrated in organized crime, their numbers and ferocity were no longer something to be scoffed at.

The trends in the older generation's way of thinking were just as unsettling: they saw the country under threat of what was later called "moral dissolution by upscale morality." In *Creative Edge: Emerging individualism in Japan,* Kuniko Miyanaga reports a rise in "individualism" resulting from Western influences, contrary to the spirit of a "group conscience" that characterized traditional Japanese culture. In his book he argues that popular belief interprets the increased crime rate as a result of "the American sickness" that will inevitably annihilate Japanese culture. [13] In the *Battle Royale* manga, this idea becomes part of the game's ideology; when the class president asks for an exemption because of his father's position as Minister of Environmental Affairs, Mr. Kamon shoots his request down with the following: "All of you are now equal in the eyes of the Program. Rich, poor, influential, downtrodden. None are exempt and why should you be?" Takami shows how easily these "Confucian ideals" can be twisted for the benefit of a totalitarian state.

Miyanaga's approach sought to focus on the sociological standpoint. The term "new men," which he used to describe those individualists, later became (unfortunately) synonymous with "detrimental emancipation."

In 2001, Kaji Nobuyuki, an academic considered head of Confucian studies in Japan, would openly state in his book *A Return to Popular Morality,* "Guide them by edicts, keep them in line with punishments, and the common people will stay out of trouble but will have no shame." [14]

In a way, this seems like a quote straight out of *Battle Royale* itself. There was a conflict brewing in Japan between the young and the old in the face of its economic crisis. For the young, the country seemed to possess no real prospects, stuck in its old ways. For the old, it seemed as if the nation was falling apart and its younger generation was to blame.

THE INCEPTION OF *BATTLE ROYALE*

In 1991, Koushun Takami dropped out of Nihon University's Liberal Arts correspondence program,[15] opting to work for the *Shikoko Shimbun* newspaper as a political, police report, and economic correspondent. He had experienced the tension between the generations firsthand, while he also reported on the decline of birthrates in the nation, both of these being results of Japan's economic crisis.

In the eyes of an imaginative man with a tendency for pessimism—an appropriate description of many writers, at least—this widening of the generational gap was a perfect basis for a fictional clash of the magnitude that *Battle Royale* hints at. While the choice might have been subconscious (a result of the ideological trend of the time) it is still the core theme of the story itself.

In the novel's iteration, Japan has become an authoritarian state, known as the Greater Republic of East Asia. It is a name strongly reminiscent of Eastasia from Orwell's *Nineteen Eighty-Four,* presenting a sociopolitical framework that could uphold such a scenario, if only barely. In the movie and manga adaptations, however, the pretense of an alternative history and alternative country is dropped. It is a skewed version of the Japanese nation, with atrocities perpetrated with the consent of its citizens. The layers are peeled back, forsaking the outdated nightmare of an all-powerful autocracy to reveal the deeper, subtler horror—the older generation is resorting to deplorable means, using the most modern measures to exterminate the young.

The young love TV shows, so *Battle Royale* is a television show. The young show a tendency for delinquency, and so most of the students are themselves juvenile delinquents. Even the law-abiding, timid ones hide a meaner, darker streak that emerges at the word "go." The old, on the other hand, are coolly under control, without acknowledging the sanctity of the lives of their sons and daughters. They maintain their façade of control, sacrificing the rebellious upstarts for the good of the nation. The old experienced the deprivations of World

War II and toiled for a better tomorrow, only to find their culture and their homeland threatened by the younger generation.

Kinji Fukasaku, the director of the film adaptation of *Battle Royale*, mentions in an interview for the Japanese cinema culture webzine *The Midnight Eye* that the movie is a "word of advice for the young,"[16] strongly reminding him of his experiences as a fifteen-year-old munitions factory worker during World War II. He even went as far as to describe *Battle Royale* itself as a "fable, a cautionary message for the younger generation," itself open to interpretation as either advice or a warning.

Battle Royale gives us an exaggerated idea of the ideological landscape of late nineties Japan. A place where—in the author's imagination—a generational battlefield emerges, where the young clash with the old, where the nation's way of life is shifting radically. Even as average workers struggle with poverty, even as the infrastructure that kept them afloat collapses. It was a time of generational warfare, and while it may appear extremely topical, it is in fact, not:

The true horror of *Battle Royale* lies in the motif of old minds sacrificing the hopes of their children and any future generations for the sake of the greater good. And to add insult to injury, the story delivers this message in the form of a highly successful, no-holds-barred competition show.

It does not offer compromise or resolution, however. All it offers is black-faced war, available on demand.

ENDNOTES

1 Braithwaite, *Poverty, Power, White-Collar Crime and the Paradoxes of Criminological Theory,* 40.
2 Nakane, *Japanese Society,* 38–40.
3 Kattoulas, "Young, Fast and Deadly: Japan's Biker Gangs," 2.
4 Taisuke and Arichika, *Japan's Challenge,* 4.
5 John D., *Violent Japanese Biker Gangs,* Tofugu.com.
6 Ikuya, *Kamikaze Biker,* 189.
7 Hayes, *Japanese Bosozoku Gangs,* FactsandDetails.com.
8 Yoder, "Youth Deviant Behavior," 136.
9 Greenfeld, *Speed Tribes,* 17.
10 Kaplan and Dubro, *Yakuza,* 133.
11 Leonardsen, *Crime in Japan,* 7.
12 Fenwick, "Youth Crime," 340.
13 Miyanaga, *Creative Edge,* 11.
14 Nobuyuki, "Popular Morality," 57.
15 "Koushun Takami," *Wikipedia.*
16 Sharp and Mes, *Interview with Kinji Fukasaku.*

BIBLIOGRAPHY

Braithwaite, John. *Poverty, Power, White-Collar Crime and the Paradoxes of Criminological Theory.* Australia: *Australian & New Zealand Journal of Criminology,* vol. 24 no. 1 (March 1991).

D., John. *Violent Japanese Biker Gangs Just Not What They Used to Be.* Tofugu website, 2012. http://www.tofugu.com/2012/03/26/violent-japanese-biker-gangs-just-not-what-they-used-to-be-bosozoku/

Fenwick, Mark. "Youth Crime and Control in Contemporary Japan." *The Blackwell Companion to Criminology,* edited by Colin Sumner. ISBN: 978-0-631-22092-3 (August 2003).

Greenfeld, Karl Taro. *Speed Tribes: Days and Night's with Japan's Next Generation.* US: HarperCollins, 1995.

Hayes, Jeffrey. *Japanese Bosozoku Gangs and Juvenile Crime in Japan.* FactsandDetails.com, 2009. http://factsanddetails.com/japan.php?itemid=814&catid=22&subcatid=147

Ikuya, Sato. *Kamikaze Biker: Parody and Anomy in Affluent Japan.* Chicago: University of Chicago Press, 1991.

Kanayama, Taisuke and Arichika Eguchi. *Japan's Challenge on the Increase of Crime in the Last Century.* Japan: Police Policy Research Center, National Police Agency of Japan, 2008. http://www.npa.go.jp/english/seisaku2/crime_reduction.pdf

Kaplan, David E. and Alec Dubro. *Yakuza: Japan's Criminal Underworld.* Los Angeles: University of California Press, 2003.

Kattoulas, Velisarios. "Young, Fast and Deadly: Japan's Biker Gangs." *TOKYO* magazine, issue cover-dated February 1, 2001. http://www.bikenet.gr/archive/index.php?topic=6325.0;wap2

Leonardsen, Dag. *Crime in Japan—a Lesson for Criminological Theory? The Cultural Dimension in Crime—What Can the Japanese Experience Tell Us?* Norway: Lillenhammer University College, 2004. http://www.britsoccrim.org/volume6/008.pdf

Miyanaga, Kuniko. *Creative Edge: Emerging Individualism in Japan.* New Jersey: Transaction Publishers, New Brunswick, 1991.

Nakane, Chie. *Japanese Society.* Los Angeles: University of California Press, 1972.

Nobuyuki, Kaji. "Call for a Return to Popular Morality." *Japan Echo,* Spotlight on Okinawa vol. 27, issue 3 (2000).

Sharp, Jasper and Tom Mes. *Interview with Kinji Fukasaku.* Archived from the original on 2002-12-05. Retrieved 2006-12-30. http://www.midnighteye.com/interviews/kinji-fukasaku/

"Koushun Takami." *Wikipedia.* (http://en.wikipedia.org/wiki/Koushun_Takami)

Yoder, Robert S. "Youth Deviant Behaviour, Conflict, and Later Consequences: Comparison of Working and Middle Class Communities in Japan." *Juvenile Delinquency in Japan: Reconsidering the Crisis,* edited by Gesine Foljanty-Jost. Netherlands: Brill's Japanese studies library, vol 18, ISSN 0925-6512.

Killer Kids in Jeopardy: Hollywood's Horror Taboo

BY GREGORY LAMBERSON

A helicopter soars over spectators. A female reporter runs toward an approaching jeep. Soldiers clear the press corps, making room for a celebrated civilian. The winner of the latest Battle Royale game has arrived: a young girl in a school uniform, clutching a stuffed animal. When she smiles, metal braces glint in the sunlight. Her eyes appear crazed, her smile that of a killer. The media swarms around her.

This chilling teaser introduced audiences to *Battle Royale,* the 2000 feature film adaptation of Koushun Takami's novel. It took three years for Takami's controversial novel to find a publisher, and then it was adapted into a manga comic book serial. Kinji Fukasaku, whose work includes *The Green Slime,* the Japanese sequences in *Tora! Tora! Tora!,* and the space opera *Message from Space,* directed the film, which his son Kenta Fukasaku scripted. After the teaser, three short scenes provide backstory for the two main characters, Shuya and Noriko, and then the story is off and running, as are the killer kids. The violence is swift, gory, and shocking, and it's no surprise the film was a hard sell in the US, which has long held an aversion to placing children in jeopardy in mainstream entertainment. *Battle Royale* didn't just broach a taboo subject—kids killing kids—it embraced it, celebrated it, and satirized it. The film is fast-paced and exhausting, with a running total of each child-on-child murder appearing on-screen like a video game. Hollywood had never seen anything like it. *Battle Royale* was the ultimate depiction of children in dramatic danger for entertainment value, both within the context of its story and in its exploitation.

Previously, most screen treatments involving adolescents in threatening situations were divided into two camps: Killer Kid movies and Kids in Jeopardy films. Adult characters generally paid the ultimate price in both categories, not kids. In the 1956 film adaptation of William March's *The Bad Seed,* little Rhoda (Patty McCormick) is a born killer, willing to commit murder over a school medal or a pair of shoes. While the offscreen death of one of her classmates launches the action, Rhoda's on-screen victims are grown-ups. In 1960, *Village of the Damned,* based on John Wyndham's novel *The Midwich Cuckoos,* presented half-alien children bent on ruling the world. Although the human siblings of these telekinetic hybrids recognize the danger early on, it's the adults who meet violent ends. One year later, *The Twilight Zone* aired a memorable adaptation of Jerome Bixby's short story "It's a Good Life," which featured godlike Anthony (Billy Mumy) wishing pesky adults into a hellish cornfield. Even in the 1970s, when supernatural kids from Niles (or was it Holland?) in Thomas Tryon's *The Other* (1972) to antichrist Damien Thorn in *The Omen* (1976) were the rage, the murderous children reserved their unholy wrath for their meddlesome elders. *Battle Royale* depicted kids killing kids with unflinching in-your-face verve, an execution that seems even more taboo in the wake of Columbine and other school shootings in the US over the last several years, but that hasn't stopped Hollywood from mass marketing the sanitized *Hunger Games* films.

Readers have taken their child characters with a salting of menace since fairy tales. Literary authors placed their child characters in jeopardy long before filmmakers followed suit. Charles Dickens loved to terrify young boys, from escaped convict Magwitch scaring Pip in the cemetery in *Great Expectations* to Oliver Twist's numerous encounters with Bill Sikes, Fagin, coffins, and dismissive authority figures. Mark Twain demonstrated no reluctance to pit Tom Sawyer and Huckleberry Finn against killers like Injun Joe. Discounting scores of live-action Walt Disney family films and the baby boomer films they inspired—*E.T., The Goonies, The Monster Squad,* and the like—and slasher films in which actors in their mid-to-late twenties portrayed teenagers, Hollywood has largely shied away from jeopardizing child characters, except when they serve as plot devices for adult heroes.

An early exception was Charles Laughton's sole turn as a film director, *The Night of the Hunter* (1955), based on the novel by Davis Grubb and starring Robert Mitchum as serial-killing preacher Harry Powell, who stalks two children down a southern river in the hope of recovering money stolen by their late father. The film is at its most suspenseful near the end of the first act, when Harry kills the children's mother, portrayed by Shelley Winters, and a drunken fisherman spots her corpse in a car at the bottom of the river. Laughton's direction becomes lyrical during the central section of the film, with the kids traveling downriver in a small boat while Harry taunts them from the bank. Laughton staged these river scenes in a soundstage, evoking fairy-tale imagery. While a classic, the film loses its edge when the kids find shelter with saintly Lillian Gish, and Harry is reduced to a comical buffoon. John and Pearl are never subjected to overt violence at Harry's hands, and the mother's murder occurs offscreen.

Distilled to its core, Takami's novel *Battle Royale* is a fusion of Richard Connell's 1924 short story "The Most Dangerous Game" and Sir William Golding's 1954 novel *Lord of the Flies.* In Connell's tale, adapted and pilfered countless times for the screen, a big game hunter washes up on an island where he finds himself hunted by a Cossack, General Zaroff, and his mute assistant, Ivan: the hunter becomes the hunted, a common theme in action films today. While Connell's story left the final confrontation to the reader's imagination ("I never slept in a better bed"), the film served up a sword fight straight out of the swashbucklers of the day. It's hard to imagine any of the deadly sport movies—*Rollerball, The Running Man, Hard Target, Surviving the*

Game, and *Battle Royale*—existing without "The Most Dangerous Game," even those based on other literary properties.

Golding's novel, adapted twice as English-language feature films, is a vaguely futuristic story set during a nuclear conflict. British schoolchildren survive a plane crash only to descend into murderous savagery on an island. Stories set on desert isles were nothing new—Daniel Defoe's *Robinson Crusoe* (1719), Johann David Wyss's *The Swiss Family Robinson* (1812), and Robert Louis Stevenson's *Treasure Island* (1883) all mined thrills from exotic island locales (with Stevenson's thirteen-year-old Jim Hawkins serving as an early example of a kid in jeopardy), but *Lord of the Flies* had bigger issues on its mind, exploring the breakdown of society, the dark side of human nature, and the loss of innocence. The children's slide into primitivism is a gradual escalation, as opposed to *Battle Royale,* in which many of the kids adopt a kill-or-be-killed mentality as soon as the adults (the real villains) send them into the jungle. The speed with which some of them become killing machines is part of the shock. In Golding's *Lord of the Flies,* the first act of murder occurs after the boys split into two camps, those led by Ralph, who wishes to preserve the rules of society, and those who follow Jack, who wants to hunt and have fun. Caught up in the frenzy of a primitive dance and convinced that tranquil Simon is the "beast" they've come to fear, the island "wild boys" bite and claw him to death (in both film versions, they use spears instead). The second murder is premeditated, with one of Ralph's soldiers leveraging a boulder off a cliff to silence intellectual Piggy. The climax finds the tribe hunting Ralph through the jungle, intent on mounting his head on a stick. People have an easier time reading about kids in jeopardy than watching them, and the novel became required reading in many US classrooms.

Peter Brook's 1963 British film is the more faithful of the two adaptations. Brook used photographs during his title sequence to suggest the nuclear conflict, and black-and-white cinematography to capture the Puerto Rican locations. The director employed a lot of zooms while moving the camera at the same time to achieve a fluid look, jumpy editing during the violent scenes, and long moments of silence to draw out suspense. Brook's techniques created a sensory and subjective point of view during Ralph's flight from Jack's hunters in the climax, and the moving shot which precedes Ralph, exhausted and crawling over sand, pulling back to reveal the gleaming white socks of a naval officer, achieved a rare cinematic quality. The film seems particularly brave for casting children who match the ages of Golding's characters, rather than aging them to ease production and audience reaction, a standard Hollywood practice. *Hornet's Nest* (1970), a US-Italian co-production, presented a new variation: killer kids as heroes. After Rock Hudson's commandos are wiped out while on a mission to blow up a dam in Italy during World War II, he is fortunate to fall in with fifteen kids seeking vengeance against the Nazis for murdering their parents. They make great trainees.

Peter Benchley and Steven Spielberg put everyone at the beach in jeopardy in *Jaws* (1975): one of the key plot points is the shark's attack on a twelve-year-old boy, and suspense is maximized when "Bruce" goes after Sheriff Brody's son a few minutes later. For the sequel, released three years later, Universal Studios ordered screenwriters Carl Gottlieb and Howard Sackler, and director Jeannot Szwarc, to place *more* kids in jeopardy, and the company got its wish.

Jonathan Kaplan's *Over the Edge* (1979) introduced the world to Matt Dillon in a tale of disaffected youth, one that applied the premise of inmates running an asylum to junior high school life. A variation of this is *Taps* (1981), in which Timothy Hutton, Sean Penn, and Tom Cruise lead an entire academy of military cadets to take over their academy and hold off the National Guard, all because their academy was about to be shut down. Hutton and Cruise assume the Ralph/Jack roles from *Lord of the Flies,* with Sean Penn standing in for Simon, and the academy for the island. Almost a decade later, the second adaptation of *Lord of the Flies* repaid the favor by borrowing military tropes from *Taps.*

Stephen King loves to put his child characters in jeopardy, and Hollywood loves Stephen King. In *Salem's Lot,* twelve-year-old Mark

Petrie becomes one of the vampire hunters who take on Count Barlow in rural Maine. In the novel, King places great emphasis on Mark's age, using it to underscore his courage and the tragedy of his witnessing the murders of his parents by Barlow. For CBS's stylish two-part TV mini-series, director Tobe Hooper appeased the network's Standards and Practices office by casting Lance Kerwin in the role. Kerwin had already starred in his own show for two seasons, *James at 15* and *James at 16.*

Stanley Kubrick faced no such restrictions when he adapted King's *The Shining* (1980) for the big screen. While eschewing many of the supernatural elements of King's novel in favor of psychological dread, Kubrick put Danny Torrance (six-year-old Daniel Lloyd) through his paces. For starters, he made Jack Nicholson and Shelley Duvall his parents. The film shifts points of view between the three main characters, and while Danny doesn't have to worry about the topiary animals from the novel coming to life, he still contends with those creepy ghost girls, the woman in room 237, and his possessed father chasing him through a hedge maze with an ax. It's doubtful any young actor spent more time portraying a child in jeopardy in one film.

Child characters are often endangered as storytelling devices. In John Cassavetes's *Gloria* (1980), a streetwise woman (Gena Rowlands) protects a young boy after the mob executes the rest of his family. The boy essentially humanizes the moll. Sidney Lumet remade the film as a bizarre feel-good film starring Sharon Stone in 1999. In Peter Weir's *Witness* (1985), Harrison Ford plays a Philadelphia detective protecting Amish boy Daniel (Lucas Haas) from corrupt cops. The first fifteen minutes of the film are from Daniel's point of view, before Ford takes center stage. Kids in jeopardy soften the hearts of even the most cynical Hollywood heroes.

Screenwriter Ian McEwan and director Joseph Ruben revisited both *The Bad Seed* and *The Omen* with their 1993 thriller *The Good Son,* in which a boy (Elijah Wood) discovers that his cousin (Macaulay Culkin) is a killer. The film departed from its progenitors by pitting child against child, providing the audience with a kid in jeopardy protagonist and a killer kid antagonist. Culkin even throws his little sister into a frozen pond to drown, but Wood rescues her. It's a slick suspense film, but in the end it is Culkin's mother (Wendy Crewson) who must make Sophie's Choice, not Wood.

Ten years later, following the international success of *Battle Royale*, the father and son duo of Kinji and Kenta Fukasaku developed *Battle Royale II: Requiem*, but Kinji died after filming just one scene, and Kenta took over. The film is a direct sequel to *Battle Royale*, but novelist Takami did not participate in its creation. In the three years since the previous film, survivors Shuya and Noriko have become the leaders of freedom fighters battling society. The film's central image shows two towers collapsing in a city of many such towers, and Shuya's group is responsible. Between production of the two films 9/11 occurred, and in *BRII*, the "freedom fighters" are terrorists who have declared war on all adults. The first half of the film is entertaining enough, with a few twists made on the original, just as TV's island-set *Survivor* reinvents its rules every season to stay fresh: this time the kids wake up collared on their school bus; they are linked in pairs so that if one is killed, the other's collar detonates; and they wear military uniforms instead of school uniforms. Shuya and his crew (but not Noriko) have holed up on another (the same?) island, and rather than attack them with true military forces, the authorities send the BR contestants to storm the mountain fortress—sort of a "fans vs. favorites" installment. The raid on the beach mimics *Saving Private Ryan* and probably matches its body count, but the pace slows when the contestants are taken prisoner by Shuya. What follows is a talky meditation on the nature of terrorism and half-assed justification for it. All adults are responsible for Shuya's deeds, but apparently American adults are more to blame (this film's teacher also blames America). In the end, Shuya and Noriko are reunited somewhere in the Middle East, don turbans, and live happily ever after. The sequel also abandoned the original film's satirical flavor in favor of its pedantic political themes.

Fans were displeased by *Battle Royale II*, and no third film was produced, unless you count *The Hunger Games* (2012), based on the novel by Suzanne Collins, published five years after *Battle Royale II*'s release. Collins has denied any knowledge of *Battle Royale* until after her novel was published, and the differences between the projects are as striking as the similarities. *The Hunger Games* is a science fiction adventure set in a future society, whereas *Battle Royale* is set in a contemporary alternate universe; Collins spends a great deal of time developing her world and establishing motivation for her heroine, Katniss, and we follow Kat through her training as she and the other kids chosen for the games become celebrities on a hit TV show. The makers of *The Hunger Games* were willing to satirize the media and notions of celebrity, but not the softened violence of the games themselves. (In *Battle Royale,* the game appears to be a secret kept from society, which makes the opening teaser with the little girl survivor swarmed by media incongruous.) Once those kids start hunting each other, the differences don't matter; the parallels are too great to ignore, with the chief difference being *The Hunger Games*' unwillingness to embrace the violence of its murder sequences (Collins's novel better approximates the brutality of Takami's vision). Collins's sequels, *Catching Fire* and *Mockingjay,* follow a similar template as *Battle Royale II*: Kat is forced to play the games again and becomes a freedom fighter perceived as a terrorist. Of course, no matter how similar the tales, the films based on Collins's novels are distinctly American while those based on Takami's are uniquely Japanese. The Fukasakus delight in making some of Takami's children alien and psychotic, while director Gary Jones tried to make even the child villains in *The Hunger Games* identifiable to viewers.

In 2006, New Line Cinema announced plans for an American adaptation of Takami's novel. One year later, in the wake of the Virginia Tech massacre, those plans stalled. In 2012, an executive for the company revealed that the success of *The Hunger Games* actually prevented the project from progressing because New Line feared audiences would consider a new *Battle Royale* a rip-off of *The Hunger Games*. That same year, the TV network the CW expressed interest in developing a weekly *Battle Royale* TV series. Several mass shootings later, said development never occurred. This is the real reason *Battle Royale* is unsuitable for mainstream America: not because we can't handle scenes of children killing kids, or scenes of gun and knife fetishism, but because those satirical portrayals hit all too close to home.

Seeing the Sequel First: Teenage Memories of *Battle Royale II*

BY ISAMU FUKUI

I had never seen *Battle Royale II: Requiem* as an adult. Before sitting down to reacquaint myself with the film for the first time since childhood, I took a moment to appreciate just how much had transpired in that intervening period. The gulf of nearly a full decade separated this viewing from the last. Having survived high school and graduated university in the interim, I was eager to see how I would receive the film with a fresh perspective. As it turns out, my first impression was that the movie did not seem to have aged particularly well—as the opening sequence finished playing, Shuya's declaration of war against "every last adult" sounded almost trite to my cynical and jaded ears. That initial reaction was enough to make me to wonder why I was ever taken with the movie in the first place. Only then did the memories of a disaffected childhood finally begin to filter through. Just like that, I could recall a time when it felt like Shuya was speaking directly to me, when his words were not hackneyed but fiercely urgent, when the movie itself felt like a reflection of my own confused and angry soul.

Even today I have nothing good to say about the public schools that I attended in my teenage years. The teachers never put an explosive collar on me, but they did not need one to force compliance. I knew that my future was being held hostage, and for that reason I dared not drop out or miss too many days of class. I shuffled through metal detectors in the mornings and allowed computers to track my movement in and out of the building. I will never forget a teacher telling me she never wanted to hear me speak in her class again, or a shriveled security guard screeching at me in broken English before having me dragged down to the principal for sitting in an empty classroom where a teacher had told me to sit. It was difficult to follow all the rules and instructions when they could be contradictory or selectively enforced; such edicts were more often the playthings of bored adults than the instruments of law and order.

A couple years ago I was invited back to speak to a class at my alma mater. On the way out I was physically tackled and threatened by a teacher who mistook me for a student trying to cut class. The administration and all individuals involved refused to apologize, indicating to me that little had changed. It had always been too much to hope that teachers, administrators, or security guards in the school might ever be held accountable for their actions. They had free rein to take out the frustration in their own lives on the students who were at their mercy. That's not to say that adults are the only bullies I remember; hazing, both ritual and otherwise, was common at my first school, where on various occasions I was strangled with a plastic bag, pelted with bricks, and shoved into a garbage can and rolled down the stairs. It was in my nature to fight back, and for that I usually ended up in more trouble than my attackers.

There were times when it felt like the yoke of education would be too much to bear, that I might snap and descend fully into madness at any minute. Worse than the daily slog itself were the isolation and doubt that I felt when I looked at portrayals of school life in fiction. The meanness and fundamental dysfunction that I saw around me was glossed over or ignored completely. Nothing I read or watched offered the possibility of meaningful change. No one seemed willing to question the status quo. This dearth of different perspectives left me feeling like I was living in a different world from everyone else, to the point where I actually began to question whether I was the only one who hated school as much as I did. It was for this reason that *Battle Royale II* would prove to be exactly the right film for me at the right time in my life.

To most other audiences, *Requiem* will never be more than an inferior sequel and the product of unfortunate circumstance. The original film was a megahit adaptation of a book by Koushun Takami. Fueled by controversy, acclaimed by audiences, *Battle Royale* became notorious even in the United States where it was almost never screened in theaters. The sequel mixed things up from the outset, offering a completely original story rather than an adaptation of the second Takami novel, which has yet to be published. However, the bigger curveball came when the director of the first film, Kinji Fukasaku, died of prostate cancer during production and passed the reins to his son and first-time director Kenta Fukasaku. The end result was not ideal. The overwhelming critical consensus (reflected by a 30 percent rating on RottenTomatoes.com) is that the second film was spoiled by its failure to live up to the sensational first. Freelance critic Nick Schager dismissed the sequel on his personal blog as "a crappy follow-up to the playfully satiric original." "Truly disappointing," wrote Miles Fielder in *Empire*. Even Jamie Russell of the BBC declared it "a disappointingly amateurish follow-up to the murderous original," and that opinion comes from one of the few critics who actually rated the sequel positively overall.

It was probably a good thing, then, that I had never seen so much as a single frame of the original film before being introduced to *Requiem* at the age of fourteen. At the time the controversy over the first movie had already made waves overseas, and although its critical reputation preceded it, I knew little about the premise other than that it involved high school students killing each other in unabashedly bloody fashion. *Battle Royale* sounded like nothing else I had ever been exposed to in my life, and so I was genuinely excited when I was offered the opportunity to see the sequel. It did not bother me much that I had never seen the first film. I care much more about such continuity issues today than I did back then.

As it turns out, that little bit of indifference would end up making all the difference when it came to my experience with *Battle Royale II,* which again, most people thought was terrible. As my introduction to the universe, the film and its complete disregard for propriety offered all the novelty that I imagine other audiences had enjoyed with the original. I had no frame of reference for a movie like this, nothing that could contextualize it or normalize it or otherwise dilute its impact. I certainly couldn't compare it to the original. To me *Requiem* wasn't retreading familiar territory or cashing in on the name of its predecessor; it was shocking and sublimely fresh from start to finish. On this, I was almost certainly alone.

A review of the available criticism online reveals a number of recurring complaints. These include the heavy-handed narrative, the sheer length (at 133 minutes the theatrical cut is a full 20 minutes longer than its predecessor), and the relative lack of suspense. Nick Schager took particular issue with the overt anti-American themes, denouncing the film as "a fundamentally misguided and repugnant piece of anti-Western civilization propaganda."

Indeed I can agree with many of those points from an objective standpoint, at least while standing here and now in the year 2014 with the full benefit of hindsight. The plot does drag at points. The story begins with the familiar sight of a Japanese class being kidnapped and strapped with explosive collars. Instead of forcing this new cast to fight each other to the death, the government sends them after the Wild Seven, a terrorist group led by Shuya, the protagonist from the original *Battle Royale.* Takuma Aoi and Shiori Kitano, the daughter of the teacher Kitano in the first film, serve as the new main characters. Almost the full first half of the film is dedicated to a bloody assault on the Wild Seven hideout on an unnamed island, and things get even more tedious after the surviving students lose their collars and join up with the Wild Seven. The subtle suspense about who will die next and how, much praised in the original film, winds up a casualty of a simplified narrative that takes turns at throwing different factions into a meat grinder while pontificating about terrorism and geopolitics.

Another casualty of the script is the characters, most of whom are rendered shallow and underdeveloped. The example of the teacher Takeuchi is a perfect case in point. As the head of the class selected for the BRII program, he is given one scene at the beginning where he explains the rules of the game and also goes on a long tangent with a list of countries that the United States has bombed over the past sixty years. Takeuchi then promptly ceases to be important until near the end when the United States threatens to bomb the Wild Seven. This imperialist intimidation upsets him, and so for some reason he is compelled to appear before the protagonists in a rugby uniform and inform them that he wished he could have played with them. He then sacrifices himself while going through the motions of an imaginary try. That last scene is more unintentionally hilarious than it is dramatic, as the narrative has not earned any serious emotional investment in the character nor does it offer any deeper subtext for the rugby gimmick. It just seems silly and a little random.

Also silly and random is the hyperbolic anti-Americanism, a theme that is pigeonholed very awkwardly into the universe of *Battle Royale*, yet emphasized too obnoxiously to ignore. While clearly a product of its time, the most damning thing about this part of the movie is that the message is muddled and shallow at best. It is embarrassing, really, to mention Japan in the same breath as Iraq in the context of American military action. As a New Yorker who was attending elementary school in the city on 9/11, I felt that the Twin Towers imagery in the opening sequence also comes off as gauche. It is clear that the filmmakers intended to offend; when questioned about the potential for controversy, Kenta Fukasaku was quoted in *Time* as saying "the more strongly people react, the better." The tragedy here is that there is room in the film for meaningful commentary on American imperialism, but either lacking the knowledge to provide it or the sophistication to try, the director instead settles for being provocative for its own sake without actually saying anything of substance. The result is one dull and uninteresting rant after another. I can only speculate that the filmmakers ended up overreaching in an effort to replicate the controversy that vaulted the original film into box office success.

That's not to say that I derived no enjoyment from the film on my recent rewatch. The once vast frontiers of extreme cinematic violence and bad taste have been explored at length by now (see *The Human Centipede* for an example of what it takes to achieve notoriety these days), and as a result there is something almost quaint about the repetitive action and bloodshed that *Battle Royale II* is so clearly proud of. In a way the film is refreshingly immature in a contemporary context. It's also somewhat unfair to suggest that professional critics found no redeeming elements in the sequel. Ilya Garger in *Time* appreciated the "idol-caliber good looks" of the main actors. Derek Elley writing in *Variety* delivered perhaps the most unreservedly positive review, calling the film "a cheeky diatribe on contempo U.S. imperialism . . . [that] does finally work, and improves on a second viewing."

None of this, however, speaks to the particular perspective I had when I saw the film for the first time. A search through the reviews available online yielded no critics who explicitly saw the sequel first, and certainly none who saw it at age fourteen. After all the years of isolation and doubt, after switching schools and finding that little had improved, for me *Requiem* was a revelation.

The film spoke to my alienation from the world as it had been hitherto presented to me. I had always struggled against the relentless efforts to convince me that modern compulsory education was a singular gift that I should appreciate and be grateful for, and that I also owed the authority figures in my life my groveling obedience and submission to their whims. I resented that perspective, but no one ever seemed to agree. *Requiem* demonstrated for the first time that it was okay to question common assumptions about the status quo, no matter how many people declared those assumptions sacrosanct. The mere fact that such a movie could exist, where the authorities were the bad guys and the insurgents were the heroes, where mistreated children could start an armed uprising and wage war on all adults, where the confidence of the establishment could be shaken by ordinary people, felt downright cathartic.

Battle Royale II, with all of its gratuitous violence and senseless cruelty, seemed to delight in presenting the aspects of humanity that I had become so familiar with but which no one wanted to talk about. I was delighted as well at the familiarity of what I saw on the screen. More than letters and numbers, high school had taught me just how mean and indifferent humanity could be. I learned that power could corrupt and that the authority figures wouldn't always have my best interests at heart. I learned that some people take pleasure in the pain of others. I learned that the strong like to prey on the weak and are often allowed to do so without consequence. I learned that there would be no arbiters of justice coming over the hill to rescue me from unfairness, only disinterested administrators looking out for their own careers. After learning all these lessons among many others, the way *Requiem* dared to illustrate the inhumanity of mankind struck a chord with me. On that island in the film I saw the same blighted moral landscape that I witnessed every day in the hallways and classrooms of my own schools.

It is likely because of that uncanny resemblance that I never found it difficult to suspend disbelief while watching *Requiem*. The premise of students being coerced into bloody combat through the use of explosive collars was less difficult to accept than the school system that commandeered my formative years and herded me like an animal into cramped rooms to passively receive information. I empathized with the students on the screen as they were sent off to do the unsavory bidding of unseen masters. The blasé manner in which the high death tolls were handled reminded me of the callous indifference with which I and others were often treated by the school system.

Much of the impact that I ascribe now to *Requiem* could just as easily have applied to the original *Battle Royale* as well, and it's difficult to say what my experience might have been had I seen the original film first. However, I do believe that it was significant that my first exposure to the universe was not the suspenseful death match between classmates in the first film but rather the ideological struggle of the Wild Seven in their violent resistance against the oppressive adult regime. The sequel offered something important that the first film did not—the possibility of fighting back against the system and changing it. The protagonists started off as helpless pawns but were ultimately able to seize control of their own destinies. This was not merely survival or subversion of the rules, but actual empowerment and revolution. That simple but electrifying concept of young people arming themselves against authority would later help inspire my first published novel.

My second journey through *Battle Royale II* proved to be equal parts nostalgic and tedious. The spark of novelty was no longer there, laying bare all the faults I knew I would find. As the film drew to a close, I watched the island get bombed into oblivion all over again. It was somewhere close to the two-hour mark when the screen faded to black. Cue the survivors reuniting in the Afghan hills in a final confused metaphor for international terrorism. My feelings were mixed as I leaned back in my seat while the credits finally began to roll. The movie did not particularly thrill me this time around, nor did it inspire any new epiphanies. I wouldn't say that it was ever my favorite motion picture, and there is no denying that much of the criticism against it remains valid and accurate. However, none of that takes anything away from the fact that at age fourteen this was a film that I had desperately needed to see.

Dead Sexy: A Defense of Sexuality in the Violently Visual *Battle Royale* Manga

BY STEVEN R. STEWART

From the moment I laid eyes on the *Battle Royale* manga, I was in love. I already knew Takami's story was great, but the manga version was *more*. Of everything. So much had been expanded, including each character's backstory, and I felt as if I knew each of them intimately. Masayuki Taguchi's precise, dynamic art oozed with character and made the daunting task of distinguishing between forty-two students in uniform not just easy, but a huge part of the fun. The illustrations brought everything to life, each tear and drop of blood, with stunning vividness. It moved me, shocked me, excited me, kept me flying through pages long after I should have been sleeping or writing or spending time with my wife. It was everything I wanted in a manga.[1]

So why did I find myself shielding the pages in public, putting the books away when parents came to visit, making sure to tell certain friends—you know the ones; we all have them—"Oh, you wouldn't like that one" before casually steering them toward the *Hikaru no Go/ Bunny Drop* section of my manga shelf?

It's not difficult to understand. *Battle Royale* is a violent train wreck of a story, and while many readers—especially my fellow Americans; the United States and violence, we go way back—might be willing to stomach a little blood and gore for entertainment's sake, throwing sex into the mix inevitably makes some people nervous. Train wrecks are fine; train wrecks with D-cups, not so much.

I love you, *Battle Royale,* but why, oh, why must you be so difficult to *defend?*

But so help me god—or whoever patronizes dirty manga—I'm about to try.

GIMMES

I suppose we could just shrug and say, "I don't see what the big deal is." But if anybody is going to accept this essay as a fair and thoughtful examination of the text, we have to acknowledge the gimmes. These are the aspects of the manga that are so offensive as to be duh-worthy, especially when taken out of context. Your mom would not appreciate, for example, hearing that a nymphomaniac abuse victim straddles a guy with a gaping gunshot wound in his torso and rides him to death cowgirl-style. That's fucked up. I know it, you know it, your mom knows it, and if we're going to defend this thing honestly, we have to acknowledge it. That's a gimme. Here are some more:

Before we've read even a single page of the manga, we're greeted by Mitsuko's panties on the title page. It's like a banner saying, "Hello, reader. More objectification to come. Hope that's cool." This, of course, is only the first in a sprawling epic sequence of Mitsuko panty shots, many of them occurring mid-murder.

Kamon, the man running the Program, flirts indiscriminately with male and female students a third his age. He makes rape jokes, kills without a thought, and at one point even drops the line "How delightfully misogynistic!" (Come on, *Battle Royale,* you're not even trying to make this easy on me.)

On the title page for Chapter 70, we see the girls from the lighthouse depicted nude—never mind that none of them are ever naked in the story—moments before killing each other off in a *Reservoir Dogs-*style bullet storm.

Then there are the gender stereotypes, in many cases reinforced by the characters' peers and parents. Kayo's mother, for example, forces her to join the floral arrangement club because it "attracts the right kind of boys." Boys are continually surprised when girls exhibit strength. Girls assume boys are "only interested in one thing."

And, of course, in a general sense, we have the problem of sex and violence. They aren't just thematic sweethearts bashfully holding hands; sex and violence are gorilla-fucking each other raw throughout the entire manga.

There's more, but I think I've dug a sufficiently bottomless hole. Let's fill it up.

COMPLEXITY

Reading the previous section, you might assume the manga is pure exploitative filth with no redeeming qualities or artistic merit. But to mangle a quote from Miss Reiko, "People [and by extension, stories *about* people] are more complex than that."

First, allow me to state the obvious: there is awful shit in *Battle Royale*, but *there's awful shit in real life too*. Violence, ugly stereotypes, sexual abuse—not everything that appears in a work of fiction is meant to be emulated; it's meant to be *weighed*. As readers, we need tragedies and cautionary tales, darkness to contrast with the light. This is one of the *Battle Royale* manga's chief triumphs: the ability to powerfully juxtapose the horrible and the beautiful, the inexcusable and the admirable, the tumultuous and the serene.

One of the best examples comes in volume 5 when Hirono is injured and thrown down a deep well. All seems lost, but miraculously, it begins to rain. The well fills up, and she swims to safety, where Shuya and the other good characters are waiting for her. They've found a way off the island. Everything is going to be all right after all. Hirono smiles and reaches for Shuya's outstretched hand—and we turn the page. (Spoiler: Hirono is not actually okay.)

Without the beauty of the first half of that scene, would we be able to feel the sense of loss we are supposed to feel at the end of it? The utter waste? What it really means for someone to lose their fight for survival? I doubt it. As readers, we need to believe the author will not protect us, that there is nothing they won't say or do, no dark corner of existence they won't show us. If we don't believe the horror of their story—if the extremes are scraped off in an attempt to make the tale "safe"—how can we believe the glorious? The transcendent? The wholly good?

THE GRAY

This isn't to say *Battle Royale* deals only in extremes. There are plenty of interesting subplots that grapple with subtler, more nuanced issues. Here are some examples if you'll allow me to get a little Socratic on you:

Does Kawada have the right idea, or is it Shuya? Is it okay to kill to protect yourself and people you love? Are you, in fact, *obligated* to kill if it's necessary for the greater good? Can mercy ever be a sin? Familiar questions, but heavy and relevant as ever.

What is the relationship between sex and death? The imagery in the manga—the Chapter 57 title page, for example, features Mitsuko completely naked except for two strands of hair and a strategically placed skull—suggests a connection, but never explicitly states what that connection is. Is it the old horror movie punishment sermon: sex is shameful, and once you've trespassed, you must be punished for sinning against your youthful vitality? Or does it have its roots in evolutionary biology? That once you've reproduced, there's nothing meaningful left to do but die? That sex itself is a risky, dangerous act? This issue has plenty of avenues for discussion if you're the analytical type. Have at it. My sex and death is your sex and death.

The manga also explores the perplexing maze of personal responsibility. The first time we meet Mimura, he's counting condoms to determine how many basketball groupies he can plow after the game. This is an otherwise kind, sensitive guy we're talking about. Does he just have a douchey streak, or could his father's womanizing example have anything to do with his actions? And if so, does that mean he's not responsible for any hurt he creates while fooling around? Shuya, on the other hand, is respectful of the opposite sex—but he had a good relationship with his mother and a strong female role model in Miss Reiko. Would he be as respectful toward women if he were in Mimura's shoes?

What about all the kids who lost their minds or killed out of fear? What about Kiriyama? He was normal before his accident, after all.

And Mitsuko. On a gut level, can you really *blame* her? In a per-verse way, isn't it almost inspiring what she does? Every man she ever trusted—with just one or two notable exceptions—treated her like meat and used her sexuality against her. So she turns it around. She reconfigures her sexuality into a weapon and a tactically brilliant one at that. Naked, vulnerable, and apparently harmless, she stupefies her victims (I'm always reminded of Gollum staring at the One Ring), and once their defenses drop, she turns *them* into meat. There is some poetic justice in that. Look at it from that perspective, and Mitsuko is not a villain, but an antihero—if you can find a way to excuse the murders of Megumi, Takako, and the like.

Rape is another difficult issue the manga touches on. As a reader, I find depictions of rape deeply uncomfortable, but it is important to realize all the characters in *Battle Royale* we are meant to respect, villains and heroes alike, have a code about sex. For example, Noriko decides to trust Shuya because he didn't peek at her panties while bandaging her leg. By contrast, the mad-dog rapists are invariably depicted as weak, ridiculous, and unlovable. And the good characters respond to them in a way that feels correct: with disgust and rage. Not a single rape victim appears to enjoy a moment of it. Takako puts up a particularly valiant fight against Niida in one memorable scene. During the attack, she recalls flashbacks of her beautiful pla-tonic relationship with Sugimura—specifically a time he told her she was difficult, but "worth the effort." She finds strength in those words, fights Niida, and wins.

There are other good examples of complex issues: The pain and awkwardness of a first sexual experience. The need to be needed. The tendency of a lonely man to look at a committed, imperfect relationship from the outside and think, "I could treat her so much better than *him*." Being simultaneously scared, dazzled, and intimidated by a partner's superior sexual prowess—and the experience it implies.

But I think you get the idea: the *Battle Royale* manga is far from mindless, exploitative filth, and there's some real depth to be found if you'll bring your brain to the reading.

BATTLE ROYALE VS. REALITY

So far, we've made the case that the graphic sexual content included in the manga has a right to be there—it carries its own weight, technically and thematically speaking—but is it *realistic*?

Let's find out.

Could someone like Mitsuko Souma even exist? RAINN—the Rape, Abuse and Incest National Network, America's largest anti–sexual violence organization—estimates that one in six women have been victims of an attempted or completed rape. That's 17.7 million women in the United States alone. More shocking, as many as 15 percent of all sexual assault and rape victims are under the age of twelve.[2] But if abuse invariably turned women into serial killers—and I don't think there's any other way to classify Mitsuko and her actions— tragically, the world would be crawling with them. In reality, only 15 percent of all known serial killers were women, just sixty-four individuals since 1826.[3]

But that doesn't mean they don't exist. And we're not just talking about so-called "Black Widow" serial killers who exclusively murder men for material gain. Fifty-one percent of female serial killers also murdered at least one woman, and 31 percent murdered one or more children. The majority were found to suffer from psychopathic tendencies and had experienced childhood abuse.[4] Sound like anybody we know?

Someone like Mitsuko could absolutely exist—admittedly, under rare circumstances—but what about her sexuality itself? In the manga, we frequently see her aroused by acts of violence and deception—and, perhaps most disturbingly, by memories of her past abuses at the hands of her stepfather. Could an abuse victim actually become sexually aroused by memories of their abuse? The answer is an unfortunate, counterintuitive, but nevertheless clear "Yes."

Psychologists have a saying: "What fires together, wires together." The human brain is a correlation machine, and when the neurons associated with pain, emotional trauma, and abuse fire alongside those related to sexual stimulation, an uncomfortable association can develop, one that can haunt a victim for the rest of their life.

Let's move on to what is perhaps the most controversial scene in the entire manga—and one I consider to be the saddest. Mitsuko almost learns to trust Yuichiro when she is captured and left in his charge, but ultimately cannot overcome her scarred mental state. Later, Yuichiro is shot trying to protect her, believing—wrongly—that she has been misunderstood and is worthy of trust. Mitsuko is so overcome with emotion—perhaps because Yuichiro is dying and it's now "safe" to have positive feelings toward him—she does the only thing she can think to do: she has sex with him. The trouble is, he's been shot, he's dying, and her unsolicited "affections" are only harming him further. It is a rape, as clear as any in the manga, one that ultimately results in Yuichiro's death.

So naturally, while reading this deeply troubling and emotional scene, the thought that kept coming to my mind was, "Wait. Can a dying gunshot victim even get an erection?"

They can, as it turns out.

Death erections—also known as "terminal erections" or "angel lust"—are a well-documented phenomenon. Pressure on the cerebellum or damage to the spinal cord has been shown to cause priapism in one out of three victims of death by hanging.[5] While hanging is by far the most common cause, priapism may also occur due to gunshot wounds, sudden brain trauma, damage to major blood vessels, or violent poisoning.

And then there's Kiriyama. Could hitting your head in an accident really turn you into an emotionless, sexually disinterested murderer-savant?

According to University of Wisconsin psychiatrist Dr. Darold Treffert, damage to the left anterior temporal lobe of the brain sometimes results in savantlike symptoms.[6] He is quick to qualify, however, that such an injury only serves to awaken dormant potential, usually a specific talent such as playing an instrument or calculating calendar dates. There have been some amazing minds awakened by traumatic brain injury (TBI), but so far an omnisavant—to coin a term right here—like Kiriyama still exists only in the realm of fiction. Loss of empathy and sexual desire, on the other hand, are very common TBI symptoms.

This is the trend we find over and over in *Battle Royale*: the truth is condensed and expanded for dramatic effect while still maintaining its roots in reality.

DON'T PLAY THE GAME

So there you have it. Yes, the *Battle Royale* manga is full of over-the-top sex and violence, but if you'll take a second look beyond your initial discomfort, beneath the blood and tears and semen, there is a hidden story full of remarkably positive themes, a story with faith in humanity at its core. In a sea of murder, we discover the only real monsters in the story are Kamon, Niida, and Oda—the rest are victims of abuse or injury, terror or mental infirmity. And while an oppressive system tries time and again to crush the human spirit, in the end, it cannot.

"I bet this happens all the time," Noriko points out. "Even with war and famine and all the horrible things in the world . . . people find one another. People learn to care." That doesn't sound like exploitative filth to me.

When it comes to bold, challenging works of art, there will always be Odas who can't see past their own sense of vulgarity, who will always be stopped by it. They'll never agree to look into anything too deeply, because they're pretty sure it's just one big sewer down there, and they can't abide the thought of a bad smell. Then there are the Yukos who just don't have the stomach for it. They're not driven by disgust or filled with contempt; they just get overwhelmed by all that intensity, and—you know what?—fair enough. If you're not a fan of *Battle Royale,* that's fine, as long as you don't make the same mistake the kids in the story make, of assuming everyone else is playing some awful game, of demonizing one another, choosing sides, picking each other apart. A person is not vulgar for finding value in something you find offensive. They're not a demon or a bad-poking kitty.

That's the game talking. Don't play.

ENDNOTES

1 Koushun Takami and Masayuki Taguchi, *Battle Royale* (Los Angeles: Tokyopop, 2003).

2 "Who are the Victims?" RAINN: Rape, Abuse & Incest National Network, accessed December 11, 2013, http://www.rainn.org/get-information/statistics/sexual-assault-victims.

3 "Serial Killer," *Wikipedia,* Wikimedia Foundation, Inc., last modified December 8, 2013, accessed December 11, 2013, http://en.wikipedia.org/wiki/Serial_killer.

4 "Serial Killer," *Wikipedia.*

5 "Death erection," *Wikipedia,* Wikimedia Foundation, Inc., last modified November 23, 2013, accessed December 11, 2013, http://en.wikipedia.org/wiki/Death_erection.

6 Darold A. Treffert, MD, "Savant Syndrome: An Extraordinary Condition," Wisconsin Medical Society, accessed December 11, 2013, https://www.wisconsinmedicalsociety.org/_WMS/savant/pdf/resources/articles/savant_article.pdf.

The Postwar Child's Guide to Survival

BY NADIA BULKIN

Disaster documentaries of the last few years have tried their best to mold us into better, faster, stronger people: *survivors,* tough enough to endure impossible hardship. The people that stumble out of the wreckage of the burning airplane, outlast the global pandemic, kill the last zombie (or terrorist). We want to believe that there is a "survivor type." Logic tells us that the answer to "who survives and why" is pretty obvious: it's the guy who does disaster preparedness training and knows where the nearest exits on the plane are. Art and media tell a different story, one encoded with societal values. American slasher movies are famous for ascribing specific moral judgments on the final girl and her dead friends—sex kills, purity triumphs. *Battle Royale,* which centers on a radical educational program that results in one winner, also presents a particular "survivor type." In fact, it presents two: that of the government that instituted the Battle Royale Act, and that of the motion picture adaptation of the novel itself. The government's model, born from Japan's fatalistic postwar depression, is perversely self-defeating; the only real way out of the horror show is following the director's handbook.

The Millennium Educational Reform Act, or Battle Royale Act, necessitates that every year one unlucky class of junior high students is sent to an island, fitted with weapons and explosive tracking collars, and told to kill each other until only one survivor is left. It was pre-cipitated by social frustration with youth delinquency. The authorities baldly describe the game as a standardized life test: "Life is a game, so fight for survival and find out if you're worth it." One thing should be made clear from the outset: this is not a movie that revels in violence for the sake of violence. But it also doesn't shy from bloodshed, as if it's something sacred. As Mitsuko says in the film, "What's wrong with killing? Everyone's got their reasons." The survivor of the game has presumably done something right, but what?

Working with friends is a feel-good answer, but it's not enough. A dying girl's smile may be interpreted to mean that she is "glad [she] found true friends," but such an interpretation primarily benefits the guilty egos of her friends. The platitudes and hopeful camaraderie also deny the stark gravity of the situation. One pointed example is the group of boys that naïvely vows that "when we escape it'll be together." They mean getting off the island, but they are all killed together instead—fulfilling their vow in a perverse way.

A more elaborate example is the group of girls that cheerfully "plays house" at the lighthouse: sharing domestic duties, cooking spa-ghetti, and generally pretending that Battle Royale is just another playground game. Reality finally interferes when an outsider, Shuya, is introduced into the mirage. An attempt to poison him through said spaghetti backfires and reveals how vulnerable their friendships are, as all the girls kill each other in a frenzy of paranoia and shock. "I even forgot that they're all my friends," says the girl that originally poi-soned the spaghetti. These efforts are met with doom not because any of them are villainous, but because of human frailty, weakness, and stupidity. "We're all idiots," says one girl. "We might have all survived." By contrast, it is notable that the three winning survivors eventually agree that, "it's for the best" if they do not stick together following the escape, because they remind each other of memories they'd rather forget. Battle Royale is an exercise in suffering, not bonding.

On the other hand, going on the offensive and killing everyone won't work either. Despite hints of the previous year's winner having reveled in killing, an enjoyment that may or may not have preceded a mental break—*"That girl definitely just smiled!"* the journalists squawk as the winner emerges with a bloody doll—uncontrolled killing sprees do not reward anyone in *Battle Royale*.

Mitsuko, a deeply wounded soul who kills, apparently, because she "just [doesn't] want to be a loser anymore," presents herself as the enemy of sentimentality. After narrowly escaping a classmate's attempt at revenge, some fragile hold on sanity inside Mitsuko clearly snaps, and she becomes a full-fledged huntress, plunging headfirst into her own revenge fantasies. When she claims that "nobody'll rescue you, that's just life," she is not only expressing her bitterness toward life but forcing her victims to feel her alienation. Mitsuko doesn't think anyone's coming to her rescue either, and it's doubtful as she stalks her classmates that she is even thinking about survival, much less life after Battle Royale. And indeed, she meets the fate she expects when she is killed by Kiriyama.

Kiriyama, for his part, is the only character with no visible inner monologue. Indeed, he does not even speak in the film. He is simply an elemental force of destruction with no origin story other than having willingly joined the game, apparently for the fun of killing others. He is therefore also the least relatable—when he is framed coming over the hill like a predator we as viewers are automatically positioned as his prey. His cold menace is the closest that *Battle Royale* comes to a traditional villain, but he does not survive either. That is, you are not meant to want to join this game. The game, like a natural disaster, is a calamity. It's to be endured, not enjoyed.

Battle Royale tells us that there is honor in fighting the system that has created this game, but the effort is ultimately futile. The tech-savvy boy gang led by the would-be revolutionary Mimura quickly grasps that their collars contain microphones through which the authorities are spying on them, and soon enough they have hacked into the authorities' computers. Mimura, it is explained, was taught how to "struggle" by his political-activist uncle and vows to exploit these vulnerabilities to bring down a repressive system.

This sympathetic group is the one real hope for active rebellion against the Battle Royale Act; if the boys had succeeded, they would almost certainly have saved some of their classmates' lives. But *Battle Royale* does not reward their boldness—they are all killed by Kiriyama, the game's inhuman force of destruction. The same fate awaits two girls who take the pacifist route and plead through a loudspeaker for the students to take up passive resistance and throw down their weapons. The Battle Royale Act forces students into an experience of annihilation reminiscent of a war. You can fight the war, and you can fight against war, but war will win.

Since the Battle Royale system cannot be fought directly, the noblest act of resistance is suicide. Two couples commit suicide, decisively marking themselves as lovers instead of fighters; the girl who poisoned the spaghetti and inadvertently caused her friends' deaths jumps from the lighthouse out of guilt. Only the poorly adjusted Mitsuko derisively says she'll "never die like that." *Battle Royale*'s true perspective of suicide is presented by Kawada, whose words take on a special significance given his status as a proven winner/survivor: "Kill yourselves together right now," he tells the protagonists. "If you can't do that, just run."

Suicide isn't survival, though. The official guide to winning Battle Royale, crafted by the government authorities that created the game itself, seems to be obedience, pep, and a certain crayon-tinted childishness—a reversion to the fascistic ideal of a young student. For the government, the model student takes to heart the condescending instructions by the woman in the introductory video: "So promise not to try that, okay?" and "As long as we're here, let's fight hard." The teacher, Kitano, demonstrates the absurdity of this cartoonish vision when he does calisthenics alone amidst the carnage.

The model student minds his or her teacher and strives to avoid this teacher's disappointment. The closest the film comes to the government's model is the only student shown any favor by an authority figure: Noriko, *Battle Royale*'s female protagonist. Shy, bullied Noriko seeks only a normal, conservative life and is girlishly sweet to everyone, including her long-suffering teacher Kitano. In return, Kitano shields her—from the rain and the brutality of the game. It is Noriko whom Kitano depicts as the final survivor in his painting littered with dead students.

But is the society that authorized the Battle Royale Act truly committed to this model student as an exemplary youth? That is, does society truly believe in the transformative value of the Battle Royale Act, or is it just a massive exercise in communal self-destruction? Another model of adult-defined success, a boy with farcical academic dedication, does vow to survive so he can "go to a good school" and is killed very early on. Unlike Noriko, this boy shows a willingness to kill his classmates—that is, to follow the instructions of the game. The Battle Royale Act is premised on mass murder, yet Noriko—the teacher's pet—is utterly passive, unable to kill (or even act!) even to save her own life. Her survival is entirely due to the actions of others obligated to protect her; she is hardly a *survivor* in any viable sense. Kitano calls her "the only one worth dying with," but she doesn't embody a reason to *live.*

This discrepancy between the authorities' model student and the nature of the game suggests that the Battle Royale Act has nothing to do with teaching students to behave or be good. It is more a reflection of the suicidal dreams of the damaged, war-torn adults who wrote the law. Noriko remarks that in her dream, Kitano "just seemed lonely," but to call Kitano depressed is an understatement. He has been attacked by his students and abandoned by his family, encapsulating the perceived breakdown of the postwar order and disruption of traditional Confucian social values.

Like Kitano, the authorities responsible for the Battle Royale Act blame the apathetic, disrespectful youth for this breakdown—they're the reason "why this country's no good anymore"—but this is a fallacious attempt to deflect blame. Adults, of course, are responsible for shaping the country and society. When Kitano snaps, "It's your own damn fault!" that the Battle Royale Act has been enacted, the students are correct to protest: "Why? What did I ever do?"

Yet Kitano is so reluctant to acknowledge his own (ir)responsibility for his own family that he shoots the telephone through which his daughter has been haranguing him about his neglect. He then encourages his favorite student, Noriko, to kill him. It is easy to imagine how *Battle Royale* is supposed to play out: Kitano and Noriko, good teacher and good student, the last of a failed society, end existence in a murder-suicide. The grown-ups, that is, have given up on this world.

Adults may blame youth because they cannot blame themselves, but everyone is intended to fall victim to the self-destruct mechanism that is the Battle Royale Act. The game has been designed to cause the most damage possible—safe zones vanish, and previous winner Kawada and trigger-happy Kiriyama are introduced to speed up the body count. Weapons allocation is random and careless—"you might get lucky, or not"—because the fortunes and miseries of life are random and careless, and everyone's bound to die anyway.

This fatalism looks absurdly pessimistic until Japan's postwar context is considered. It may seem strange to think about "postwar Japan" in the year 2000, but Japan has been mired in a postwar state since the American occupation. The adults of *Battle Royale*—babies when Japan surrendered—inherited a tainted, tired nation that had not only lost World War II, but been met with universal condemnation for its wartime actions and blasted with the deadliest bomb ever invented. The occupation and castration of the military reinforced the sense of national victimhood and helplessness. "Calling for peace was a good idea," Kitano admits, with no small amount of regret. "Can't win 'em all."

Following the war, Japan focused its efforts on modernization and industrialization through economic development and an efficient political system. On the surface, Japan's rehabilitation was hailed a major success. But Kitano's generation never got out of the shadow of defeat.

In the early 1990s, Japan's wonder economy began the deflationary recession it still hasn't fully emerged from. In "Japan's Long Postwar:

The Trick of Memory and the Ruse of History," Harry Harootunian points out that 1995 not only marked the fiftieth anniversary of the Japanese surrender, but was ominously punctuated by two major disasters: the Hanshin earthquake, which revealed the failure of early-warning systems and supposedly earthquake-proof engineering, as well as government incompetence; and the Aum Shinrikyo sarin gas attacks in the Tokyo subway, the most notorious instance of Japanese domestic terrorism.[1]

The seeming failure of the education system to produce a nation of well-mannered, high-achieving adolescents only confirmed what the postwar generation already knew: society was breaking down. This failure manifested in a variety of ways, from the mundane—bullying, delinquency—to the extreme—teens who won't leave their rooms, and worse, Boy A (1997) and Girl A (2004), children who killed other children. Their pseudonyms are eerily similar to *Battle Royale*'s referring to the dead teens by number (*"Boys, Number Four"*).

Boy A murdered a younger boy and left the decapitated head at the gates of his school in what he claimed was an act of protest against the school system. He was quite clearly a sociopath with a track record of abusing children and animals, but the press seized upon the shocking crime to force Japan to undergo its own national standardized exam: "Where did we go wrong?"

Postwar social conservatives blamed senselessly violent media and a school system that evidently wasn't building a functional moral compass. To fix this, the Central Council for Education suggested a little bit of moral indoctrination—namely, reprioritizing traditional family values: "Let us prize the influence of fathers, let parents read books to their children and let children share household chores with their parents."[2] It's a reactionary solution that echoes earlier attempts to reinvigorate Japan by instilling an energetic nationalism through less depressing, and less accurate, textbooks. This is the Noriko method: survival through the enthusiastic reinforcement of traditional social roles.

This eagerness to get back to a pure Japan where children respect their elders, look after their juniors, and clearly differentiate right from wrong—and no one needs to feel ashamed and defeated—has fascistic undertones that have not been lost on observers. It's as if certain segments of the postwar generation don't know of any other way out from a corrupted society than taking up the prewar fascism that originally brought them to their postwar depression. As *Battle Royale* shows, the Noriko method doesn't actually work if one's objective is indeed survival. It leads to only one outcome: mutually assured destruction.

But just because the authorities have designed the Battle Royale game to fail does not mean that no survivor emerges. The authors of *Battle Royale*—in this case, director/screenwriter Fukasaku—have their own version of a model student that is quite distinct from that of the in-universe authorities. The authorial vision of a survivor is dedicated, stalwart, and resilient. The real hero of *Battle Royale* is not Noriko at all; it's Shuya, a boy who has kept on surviving after his parents, in his words, "ran off or died because they felt like it."

Unlike Noriko's rose-colored view of society and social order, Shuya has felt the full impact of the older generation's failure to take proper responsibility for the nation. As *Battle Royale* opens, his father has killed himself, likely out of shame over his inability to find employment. "I say go for it," his father once told Shuya, "but I never taught you anything." His mother has long since deserted him, and he is placed in an orphanage. Confronted with the absurdity of Battle Royale, Shuya professes, "I don't know what any of it means!" He does know, however, what Kawada warns him of: "It's going to be tough going."

Shuya is armed, but his main strategy is simple: running. After Shuya, Noriko, and Kawada escape the island, Kawada—another proven winner—tells Shuya to "just keep going straight and you have to hit land." Fighting the system does not work; neither does bonding with a large group of friends, much less attacking a large group of friends. Endurance—at any cost, and without understanding—is the only option. Shuya's difficult childhood no doubt prepared him for this; unlike Mitsuko, however, Shuya has not lost the ability to show compassion for others and is able to ground his misery in reality.

While Mitsuko loses her self-control in her own neurosis, Shuya is able to skate along the surface of his consciousness—to literally move past situations without dwelling long enough to get lost in them. Whether this is due to Shuya's lacking depth and intelligence or his pragmatism, it is impossible to say. Perhaps running without thinking is the only rational response to the orgy of self-destruction. Shuya would seem to think so, intoning near the end of *Battle Royale* that "we've got no choice but to keep moving forward." The only thing directly demanded by the game itself, after all, is constant movement across the terrain.

The idea of the running youth complicates a common criticism of *Battle Royale*: that the ideal female student (Noriko) is passive, while the ideal male student (Shuya) is active. This critique contrasts the guileless, hapless Noriko with the manipulative, ruthless Mitsuko. But there is another major female character, the real "heart's darling" of *Battle Royale*: Chigusa. Chigusa is both active and passive, both a "good girl" and "bad girl." She kills a boy pressuring her to have sex with great violence, sporting a yellow jumpsuit like Bruce Lee's in *Game of Death* and, a few years later, Uma Thurman's in *Kill Bill*. Chigusa is a dedicated track star and thus the best runner of them all. The authorial love and respect for her is evident—she is described by the boy she loves as "the coolest girl in the world."

The fact that Chigusa doesn't survive despite embodying the model of running (she is killed by bad girl Mitsuko) suggests that she is somehow too much, too quick to kill, too solemn of a thinker, too emotionally stunted to be honest with her only friend. She runs so fast that even the boy she loves "called [her] but couldn't catch up." Shuya's personality, on the other hand, is tempered by his closeness to his friends and his angst over killing. He's more average—more human— than Chigusa the Valkyrie. He even describes himself as "weak" and "useless." But you don't need to be a hero to survive Battle Royale. You just need to keep going. It sounds simple, but as any survivor of a real disaster can attest, the ability to keep level in a high-stress situation is underrated and hard to come by.

Ultimately, Noriko and Shuya represent two very different value systems, not masculinity and femininity. Noriko is the non-viable model chosen by the fatalistic in-universe authorities, and Shuya is the viable model crafted by the creators of *Battle Royale*. His top characteristic as a survivor is his ability to keep the ground beneath his feet, to endure the abandonment and societal destruction of the demoralized adults.

The powers-that-be may have given up on the war-torn world, left believing that catharsis will come at the edge of a knife. Having children destroy one another is the surest way to destroy the future— but they have underestimated the postwar child's capacity for biting down and grinding through the bloodshed. *Battle Royale*'s survivor model knows how awful this game is, and instead of trying to master it or defeat it, the survivor runs from it. In *Battle Royale*'s last words, Shuya instructs his audience, his voice stark against a black screen: "No matter how far, run for all you're worth. Run!"

ENDNOTES

1 Harry Harootunian, "Japan's Long Postwar: The Trick of Memory and the Ruse of History," *The South Atlantic Quarterly* 99, no. 4 (2000): 715–739.

2 Takahashi Shotaro, "When Student Violence Erupts," *Japan Quarterly* 45, no. 3 (July 1998): 77–83.

Children Playing with Guns

BY BRIAN KEENE

There is an early scene in the film version of *Battle Royale* in which a shotgun-wielding Kawada confronts Shuya and Noriko and demands to know what kind of weapons they've received. Shuya sheepishly displays an innocuous pot lid, and Noriko is armed with a simple pair of binoculars. Kawada shakes his head, obviously bemused.

Battle Royale is full of weapons—automatic submachine guns, double-barrel shotguns, axes, hatchets, stun guns, bombs, and even a ludicrous paper fan. Most of these weapons are used at some point throughout the film, but it is the scenes depicting the non-gun violence that are among the most graphic and disturbing. Killing a fellow student with an Intratec TEC-DC9 or a Hi-Point 995 carbine can be done from a distance, thus allowing the killer to somewhat disassociate themselves from the act. Murdering a classmate with a machete or an ice pick requires a more personal involvement—the bloodying of one's hands, in a very literal sense. Shooting someone from seventy-five yards away keeps the brain matter off your boots. Stabbing them up close with a knife means you're close enough to smell the very particular stench that wafts from a fresh gut wound.

In the hands of a determined killer, anything can be a weapon. The adults in *Battle Royale* knew this, as evidenced by the selection of weaponry they bestowed upon the unlucky students of Class 3-B. And I knew it myself as a teenager in the early eighties, when Frank Miller's seminal run on Marvel Comics' *Daredevil* introduced an entire generation to the ways of the ninja. My friends and I spent an entire summer obsessed with ninja—saving money from our paper routes and allowances to order books and pamphlets offering "The Secrets of Ninjutsu" from the backs of our fathers' copies of *Soldier of Fortune* magazines. Because ninja supposedly had the ability to turn anything into a weapon, we would often play a game, pointing out innocuous, common household items to each other and asking how we'd turn them into weapons. (My pals thought they had me when they suggested a sheet of typing paper, until I decided that you could use it to deliver a paper cut to someone's jugular vein).

My friends and I, it should be noted, were all normal (if somewhat hormonal) teenage kids. We may have listened to too much Iron Maiden and Black Flag, but none of us ever embarked on a shooting spree. Instead, we grew up to be parents and doctors and steelworkers, and, in my case, a writer.

It should also be noted that each of us knew our guns. I grew up in a small Pennsylvania paper mill town. Most years, it seemed like the union was on strike, which meant that funds were tight. Almost all of the families I knew supplemented their groceries and their government cheese handouts by hunting, and we were no strangers to venison, rabbit, or wild turkey on the table instead of Ballpark Franks. Hamburger Helper, it turns out, goes just as well with squirrel as it does with hamburger.

I learned to hunt when I was fourteen, and when I shot my first deer, I learned that I didn't have the stomach or conscience to be a hunter. Some of my friends discovered the same thing about themselves. Others took to hunting with zeal. But all of us knew how to shoot. More importantly, we knew how to safely handle a firearm. Hunting was so widespread in our community that we had classes in middle school on firearm training and safety. The first, and most important, safety tip was this: **lock your guns up so your kids don't**

have access to them. And our parents did just that. In our households, we only handled those weapons with direct parental supervision. We played with toy guns, but we never played with real guns.

In today's culture, according to the plethora of gun laws on the books in most states, it is supposed to be harder for teenagers to gain access to firearms, and yet, in case after disturbing case, we hear of them obtaining such weapons with ease. Seung-Hui Cho, the college student who killed thirty-two people at Virginia Polytechnic Institute and State University, was able to legally purchase a number of firearms despite being diagnosed with several psychiatric disorders as far back as middle school, two previous stalking complaints by female students, and a history of abnormal behavior that concerned both family and friends. Sandy Hook Elementary shooter Adam Lanza obtained his guns at home, many of which were gifts from his mother, who encouraged his firearms training during trips to the local shooting range, despite a similar background to Cho's. Eric Harris and Dylan Klebold, the infamous teenaged Columbine gunmen, were able to obtain their weapons through straw purchases made by adult friends, paid for with money Harris earned working part-time at a local pizza shop.

So, obviously, the common denominator is guns. Except that it isn't. Just like Class 3-B in *Battle Royale,* the arsenal of Columbine's Harris and Klebold's wasn't limited to firearms. The two had manufactured several different kinds of homemade bombs and pyrotechnics, as well as amassing a collection of knives and other nonexplosive weapons. The preteen killer in Japan's Sasebo elementary school used a common utility knife. The juvenile murderer in Japan's Kobe slayings used a hammer and a hacksaw on his victims. When Charles Carl Roberts besieged an Amish schoolhouse in rural Pennsylvania, his auxiliary weapons included chains, plastic ties, and a tube of K-Y sexual lubricant. And in the case of the Bath School massacre, a bomb and other improvised explosives killed thirty-six children and two adults.

In all of these cases except for the latter two, the massacres involved youth killing other youth. In *Battle Royale,* it is former teacher Kitano and his military cohorts who arm the students prior to turning them on each other. Can the same be said of these real-life cases of child-on-child murder? Perhaps not maliciously, but does gross parental irresponsibility (such as in the case of Adam Lanza's mother, Nancy) not equate to the same thing? In some cases, possibly. It's natural for us to wonder what Nancy Lanza was thinking, encouraging her emotionally disturbed teen to take up firearms and go target shooting with her. We can't ask her, since she was Lanza's first victim, shot in the head four times while lying in bed. But we can wonder. Was she aware that she was arming him for a massacre to come? Or was she simply a stressed-out single mother, trying to do the best for her special needs child, a child who had trouble connecting with others? Did she find that connection through target shooting, a pastime enjoyed by hundreds of thousands of responsible parents and teens throughout America?

Or what of Eric Harris, whose basement bedroom was filled with explosives, detonators, ammunition, and bomb-making equipment? Were his parents culpable in arming him, simply by not going into his bedroom and finding such materials? Was the local sheriff's department equally responsible by preparing a draft search warrant for his home after learning Harris and Klebold had been fashioning pipe bombs and threatening their classmates—but never formally filing the search warrant or following up on the claims?

Perhaps not. No parent wants to consider the possibility that their child is a murderous psychopath. Indeed, few parents even know what warning signs to look for. Focusing on greater mental health care and awareness is a good start. But so many of those "warning signs" are behaviors seen as normal in our everyday teen society. A fascination with violent video games, comic books, movies, or literature? Lock up 90 percent of our youth. A fondness for heavy metal or gangsta rap? Ditto. Weaponry? What about those kids like me and my friends, hunting with our fathers or playing with ninja throwing stars we bought at a flea market for a buck a piece? We didn't take those throwing stars to school and begin puncturing our classmates with them. At worst, we impaled a few trees.

Despite the plethora of plain-sight evidence against Harris, most of his classmates and teachers described him as bright, friendly, and outgoing. His accomplice, Klebold, seemed "nice, but shy. Kind of quiet." To many of their victims, they seemed like normal kids, until the killing started—just like the children of Class 3-B. Sure, we learn early on that Mitsuko is a sociopath. (In an extended-cut version of the film, it is revealed that her murderous tendencies are rooted in an earlier attempted molestation at the hands of her mother's boyfriend, whom Mitsuko pushes to his death down a flight of stairs.) And sadistic transfer student Kazuo Kiriyama is certainly no stranger to killing. Indeed, he seems to revel in it. But the vast majority of the kids in *Battle Royale* are just that—kids, normal teenagers who are suddenly armed by adults and told to slaughter each other. Because it's the law.

It is easy to point to America's gun laws and argue for more restrictions. But the fact remains that in almost every case, the culprits obtained their guns either by circumventing the very laws designed to safeguard against such atrocities or through the adults in their lives. While an argument for stricter gun laws can certainly be made (and should be discussed—calmly, rationally, and without the hyperbole from both the Left and the Right)—the fact remains that such laws would not have prevented these massacres from occurring. Nor would they have stopped the culprits in the Kobe murders or the Bath bombing or so many other cases.

So, what then, are we to do? If enforcement of current gun laws or the passage of yet stricter laws won't help, and if parents can't responsibly assess and identify whether their child may be at risk of committing such heinous atrocities, then what are we to do?

Is it possible that *Battle Royale,* like the best dystopian science fiction, is a dark precursor of what's to come—a prediction of what lies ahead for our children and our society? Could it be the antithesis to The Who's statement that "the kids are all right"?

During *Battle Royale*'s climax, a mortally wounded Kitano tells his daughter, Shiori, that "If you hate someone, you take the consequences."

As a parent, I've taught my children to always stand up for themselves and those they care about, and to never, ever tolerate a bully, be it a classmate or some aspect of the system itself. But I've also taught them not to hate. I like to think I've succeeded—that they don't view others in terms of race or gender or faith or sexual preference. I've tried to teach them that love is the answer to all things, and that the only things that deserve hate are ignorance and oppression. I hope that I have armed them, not with machine guns or axes or pot lids, but with compassion and reason.

But every morning, when I drop my five-year-old off for another full day of kindergarten, and I watch until he goes inside and disappears from my sight, I'm left wondering what lessons his classmates are learning at home, or from each other, or from our society, and what the consequences of those lessons might one day be. I wonder what they're being armed with, and what weapons are in their arsenals, and if compassion and reason and love are an equal match.

And then, I wait for the school day to be over so I can hold him again.

List, Combination, Recursion

BY TOH ENJOE

TRANSLATED BY JOCELYNE ALLEN

There are many legends about *Battle Royale*. Because they're legends, I don't know if they really happened or not, and there's honestly not much point in fact checking. The important thing is that these legends continue to be told even now.

For instance, there's this one.

Battle Royale was once banned. The selection committee members for the Japan Horror Novel Award, to which *Battle Royale* was submitted, decided to bury this work because the content was simply too antisocial. While they were at it, they decided to hit the switch on the bomb in the collar. The author was dead.

But the author lived. (As to how, people who have read the book will know.) Quiet rumors made the whispered rounds, and there even appeared an underground publisher willing to brave the dangers inherent in bringing the work forth into the world. But information on the author and the manuscript was firmly suppressed.

The publisher took out an ad in its own magazine soliciting information on the writer (an ad, which no doubt, most certainly contained some sort of secret code as well). At which point, the author himself contacted them via secret channels, and in this way, the dream of seeing the story brought to life as a book came true.

There's also this legend. According to a certain member of the selection committee, *Battle Royale* "surpassed the limits of the novel and killed too many people." Thus, a written agreement was established: "The number of murder victims within a single novel must stop at no more that eight."

And then there's this story. An argument occurred in the Diet that there must be consequences for such an antisocial publication being released upon the world. (Perhaps to defend and maintain the national polity of the Republic of Greater East Asia.)

Battle Royale has already been the object of much critical work. Some have declared the pleasure of the work as simple entertainment (so don't start grumbling about that), and some have said that it delineates the real world or the actual existence of young people (in other words, it is a mouthpiece and a prophet). If some criticism laid out the beauty of the vulgarity, others emphasized the sadness of how powerless we are in the face of the physicality of humans, of humans that are nothing but physical, and called it a written social experiment, a thought experiment. "The war of all against all"; *Of the Social Contract, Or Principles of Political Right; And Then There Were None; Lord of the Flies;* game theory; *The Long Walk.* They killed people like it was a game. Likely the influence of horror movies and Nintendo.

All of these arguments include perceptive viewpoints, but overall, they betray a thickheaded grudge. You cannot deny the narrowness of perspective somehow when it comes to *Battle Royale.* Which is why I want to here draw out several additional lines overlaying and penetrating this work.

At the beginning of *Sade, Fourier, Loyola, Battle Royale,* Roland Barthes wrote, "From Sade to Fourier, sadism is lost; from Loyola to Sade, divine interlocution; from Fourier to *Battle Royale,* the ideal." Well naturally, Barthes never wrote any such book, but I don't feel like spelling the whole thing out. From people who say they like *Battle*

Royale, I'd expect that a certain level of cultivation is simply a matter of course. *Sade, Fourier, Loyola* is, in other words, a text on the classification of evil influences, stating that generally classified items that grow toward excess immediately and are put to unexpected uses give rise to repeated acts of madness. What Barthes discovers in *Sade, Fourier, Loyola* is listified to the point of obstinacy; the actual human being is promptly erased here, changed into symbols and numbers, and a numbered order appears. It is a social order imagined as the ideal prior to a controlled society and all that which starts already with violence before it even exists.

Let me here remind you of Kurt Vonnegut's *Galápagos.* The characters in this novel have an asterisk placed in front of their names as they approach death. In Naoki Yamamoto's *Red,* a number appears written on the sides of the characters' heads, showing the order in which these people are going to die. You, having finished reading *Battle Royale,* can now see numbers floating up next to the names on the class register. All of which is to say, they are listed and ordered. This is a place where the alphabetized list and the death-order list (perhaps I should say naturally) intersect violently.

The madness brought about by the listing required for ordering easily becomes rampant. Come up with a separate list and add it to the pile above you. That is, ordinary characters in a novel are essentially lined up as characters, and it wouldn't be strange at all if from the moment they appear they were to ignore the author's intentions and expectations and at some point begin killing one another. To put it another way for people who are slightly anxious about their intelligence, the space which makes possible the imagining of the characters and the enactment of the text is already simultaneously set up as the foundation on which a massacre can be born. Due to the fact that this is the space that rules the order called literature, it always runs the risk of excess and violence. The characters are literature and so they do not die; they also do not feel pain. And naturally, because this ordering is possible, people are able to actually kill people, and it is even possible for them to imagine that their victim does not feel pain.

The relationship between Japanese people and listing is unexpect-
edly old. If nothing else, the technique of "enumeration" had already
been established in the period of the lesser councilor of state Sei, a
personage from the tenth century. In the section "Killing" included in
her *Pillow Book,* we find, "When killing people, the use of a knife is
quite banal; a scheme with a rope is more elegant. To gouge out the
eyes with the bare hands requires a certain skill, while stabbing with a
sickle is deeply refined. A beating with a belt is unsightly, and shooting
with a machine gun lacks grace. A pistol is good to keep from dirtying
one's hands, but for total domination, it loses to the shotgun—"; this
continues on at length. Again, I ask you to pay attention; I would like
that readers please be equipped with cultivation and common sense.

This technique of enumerating things such that they are essentially stripped of meaning would still have life in the history of Japanese
literature even after the appearance of *The Pillow Book,* and be woven
into the hearts of the Japanese people, splitting off and showing its
face here and there. We can perceive this technique in such things as
the *michiyuki* (introductory traveling scene) of Noh. These scenes are
nothing more than dialogue overlaid on a travel route; in the Noh song
"Round-Robin" (er, this song naturally doesn't exist, but I can write it
down if you like), the lead actor starts with a line like this: "0308AM;
G=07, 0700AM; J=02, 0900AM; F=01, . . ." It is obvious that this
is already forming the flow of the river that pours into *Battle Royale.*

However, it is also a fact that in Japan, the technique to juggle combinations as if engaging in a form of play with possible arrangements of
combinations has long lay dormant underground from modern times
and on. The number of people who have made free use of listing and
enumeration techniques prior to the appearance of *Battle Royale* is a
count of just one, Futaro Yamada. Of his many works, this is especially
remarkable in the *Ninpocho* ninja series. In *The Kouga Ninja Scrolls,*
representative of the series, a family of ninja living in the Iga and Kouga
districts fight a ninja battle in which the ten representatives, facing off
against ten rival representatives, bathe the scene in blood. While some
fights are direct because of ninja fighting capabilities, there are also

some that don't seem to serve any purpose at all at first glance. But these fighting skills are intrinsic, and it doesn't do any good to insist on advantages or disadvantages. What we should pay attention to is this: the majority of his *Ninpocho* series use team battles. In other words, he makes use of every possible variation of ninja technique, with the fighting carried out combination style.

And Futaro Yamada himself had this to say about the theme of slaughter:

> So if you try to rationalize things somehow, there's nothing in this world that can't be rationalized, and nowadays, pretty much everything is explained away. You grab an adjective to stick on, like "alone" or "heartless," like a single memory or something, and you plan to tie it all together, which just makes me burst out laughing. Why can't we just enjoy it as harmless nonsense? If the ninja arts have a connection to modern times, it's that they are distant from modern times.
>
> (Ninja from *Kasshiyawa*)

Just as sonnets, haiku, and *lushi* poems do not yet have meaning from the structure alone, team battles and battles royale also do not generate meaning from just their structures. They don't even yet mean nothing. These are just vessels. And with a vessel, you should, in fact, put something in it. It's not the case that the decision has been made that you must put liquids in a cup. You're free to simply pour pleasure in it if you want, and that is normally called literature.

The combinations realized by the team battle and enumeration have been updated in this way by *Battle Royale,* but a complete battle royal state has yet to be achieved. Because, simply put, what starts up after the end of *Battle Royale* is a team battle of government versus antigovernment.

Although it's unclear how this battle played out, we actually have one clue. The existence of this *Battle Royale* is one piece of evidence. Suppose this text was a depiction of the real world—it would be impossible for the book to have been published in this reality. And in addition to us not yet having witnessed this spectacle as something from the real world, we can make one further inference. *Battle Royale* is a spectacle we will witness in the future. And we will one day be subjugated by its reality. A world in which *Battle Royale* can exist again will be restored. As if the novel *Nineteen Eighty-Four* had never been written in the world of *Nineteen Eighty-Four*.

Bueller, Bueller, Do You Read? Random Notes on *Battle Royale* and the American Teen Film

BY SAM HAMM

LOGLINE: *In an effort to control its rebellious population, an authoritarian government rounds up adolescents, drops them into an isolated setting, and forces them to fight to the death until only one remains. These gladiatorial games are a media sensation, and winners—that is, survivors—are treated as national celebrities. During each contest, ad hoc alliances form, often based on pre-existing friendships or hitherto unexplored "crushes." Most participants are killed in gaudy fashion after demonstrating exploitable weaknesses or character flaws. Some sacrifice themselves so that others might live. In this year's contest, however, there is an unprecedented twist. Our protagonists, the last survivors, refuse to kill one another, violating the rules and undermining the very purpose of the games. Love triumphs, but at a cost: the winning couple must now face the institutional wrath of the corrupt regime they have defied.*

As you know, I am describing the American box-office blockbuster *The Hunger Games* (2012), directed by Gary Ross and based on Suzanne Collins's hugely popular novel of 2008.

As you know, I am also describing the Japanese box-office blockbuster *Battle Royale* (2000), directed by Kinji Fukasaku, and based on Koushun Takami's hugely popular novel of 1999.

You're reading this book, so in all likelihood you're thinking to yourself that the former is a cheesy rip-off of the latter, even though Suzanne Collins has repeatedly claimed that she'd never heard of *Battle Royale* before completing her book, even though Koushun Takami has given her his (rather grudging) public absolution: "Every novel has something to offer . . . [if] readers find value in either book, that's all an author can ask for."[1] Still: look at the plots. Look at the dates. Surely, given the similarities, one international phenomenon must have, at the very least, *influenced* the other.

Okay. Now tell us something we *didn't* know.

All movies steal from other movies. Genre movies steal from other movies, but they do it openly—avidly, even. When a particular "type" of movie catches on with a mass audience, its constituent elements—tropes, settings, "looks," plot movements, character archetypes—will be recycled and recombined in subsequent films, as other filmmakers attempt to duplicate and improve upon the successful "formula" of the original(s). When the process takes place many times over, a genre emerges.

Once the conventions of the genre are established, filmmakers begin to tweak the conventions. Every genre film is engaged in a playful dialogue with its genre, and it's here, in the interpolations, the interrogations, the little subversions, that audiences find their deepest pleasures, as when a jazzman discovers something startling and fresh in, let's say, "My Favorite Things" and totally reinvents the song. It is not hard to write a loose synopsis that would describe both an Anthony Mann Western with Jimmy Stewart and a Budd Boetticher Western with Randolph Scott, although the experience of watching them is quite different; if you saw them both on a double bill, you might barely notice the overlap. *Sultry dame lures smart guy into get-rich-quick scheme; the sex is hot until the plan goes south and the two of them turn on each other.* Quick: which *film noir* am I describing? Most of them, is the answer. Yet most of "most of them" offer their own distinct and idiosyncratic gratifications, their own *frissons*.

Even the most venerable plots look fresh when you dress them up in a new genre coat. *Red River* is *Mutiny on the Bounty*, with the action moved to a cattle drive. *Forbidden Planet* is *The Tempest* relocated to Altair-4. *Sons of Anarchy* is *Hamlet* in a motorcycle gang. *Alien* is *It! The Terror from Beyond Space* with a budget. You can also tart up a familiar story by kicking it a few time zones to the east or west; just check out Akira Kurosawa's frequently plundered filmography for proof. Sergio Leone's *A Fistful of Dollars* is an uncredited Italian remake of AK's *Yojimbo*, with many sequences reproduced shot-for-shot. *The Magnificent Seven* is *Seven Samurai; The Outrage, Rashomon; Star Wars* is, if you squint hard enough, *The Hidden Fortress.* (It goes both ways, of course. While Western filmmakers were "borrowing" from his action pictures, Kurosawa was busy importing Shakesepeare and Gorky and Dostoevsky to Japan. I would be remiss not to mention that the plot of *Yojimbo* is a straight lift from Dashiell Hammett's *Red Harvest.*)

So yes, *The Hunger Games* is "influenced," maybe even infected, by *Battle Royale*. But what films influenced *Battle Royale?* There's a long tradition of movies about humans hunting humans, many of them based, officially or unofficially, on Richard Connell's short story "The Most Dangerous Game," and a shorter list of movies—often explicitly satirical—about legally sanctioned mayhem as public spectacle: *The 10th Victim* (from a Robert Sheckley story), *The Running Man* (from a Robert Sheckley story As Retold By Stephen King), *Death Race 2000, Rollerball, Series 7: The Contenders,* and *The Condemned,* among others. At first glance, the most original element of *Battle Royale* would seem to be the age of its cast—you rarely see junior high students in mortal combat.

The kids versus kids premise is almost universally read as a metaphor for the intense competitive pressures facing the schoolchildren of Japan, where rigorous entrance exams weed out the less gifted, and the less industrious, at an early age. Many parents make great financial sacrifices to send their middle-schoolers to *juku,* or "cram school," in hopes of boosting their scores; those who fail to make the grade are thought to have shamed their families. A lot of them kill themselves.

Americans who read about the annual spike in Japan's teen-suicide rate are no doubt shocked to learn that any culture could place so high a premium on education.

Not that the American high school is an especially congenial venue in which to pass one's postpubescent years. The academic demands may be relaxed by Japanese standards, but the social pressures are just as great, with various cliques and demographic affinity groups as rigidly stratified as any you'd find in the state penitentiary. There is great pressure to conform to the social and physical demands of other kids who are bored, horny, and not infrequently vicious toward their social inferiors. Many of them have recently made the acquaintance of drugs, booze, and sex. Look at a sampling of movie titles from the seventies and early eighties: there's *Horror High* (1974), *Massacre at Central High* (1976), *Class of Nuke 'Em High* (1986), *Slaughter High* (1986), *Return to Horror High* (1987), *Monster High* (1989), and *Cemetery High* (1989), not to mention *Prom Night* (1980), *Graduation Day* (1981), etc. Somebody somewhere had obviously realized that, for an audience of youthful ticket-buyers, high school and horror went hand in hand.

While poring over the list above, I began to wonder whether a loose cladistic analysis of narrative DNA might reveal unexpected similarities between *Battle Royale* and the American high school movie, or at least locate the two on nearby branches of the constantly proliferating Bush of Genre. What follows is a brief and necessarily impressionistic account of that research. The fools at the academy will think me mad. So let 'em.

For the purposes of this discussion we will examine American high school movies released in the three decades or so prior to *Battle Royale.* The high school movie, it seems to me, falls into four distinct subgenres:

1. **The Inspirational Drama** (*Lean on Me, Stand and Deliver, Dangerous Minds,* etc.; obvious precursors include *The*

Blackboard Jungle and *To Sir with Love*), in which a dedicated teacher uses empathy/humor/discipline/tough love to change the lives of students whom the system has discarded as irredeemable. *BR* is, if anything, a rebuke to the assumptions of the Inspirational Drama. Ex-teacher Kitano (played by the distinguished action director and star Takeshi Kitano) does change the lives of his former students, but well, not like that. Kitano himself is explicitly a reference to the teacher protagonist of the televised Japanese inspirational drama *Kinpachi Sensei.*

2. **The Tale of Sexual Initiation,** in which one or more (usually) male protagonists loses his virginity, (usually) in comic fashion, (usually) in the company of a prostitute or a lonely older woman he has mistaken for a prostitute. The TSI is often set in period to give its target demographic a reassuring sense that sexual awkwardness, like polio, has been successfully eliminated from the modern world. Early entries in the cycle are marked by a certain gauzy wistfulness (*Summer of '42, The First Time, Jeremy*), but after the success of *Porky's* and its sequels, the subgenre devolves into straight raunch (*Private Lessons, Private School, Private Resort, My Tutor, The Last American Virgin*), with occasional digressions into slightly tonier territory (*Losin' It, Class*). *Fast Times at Ridgemont High* represents the road not taken. Outliers include distaff variations, such as *Little Darlings* and the brutish *Last Summer; The Last Picture Show,* too big for the genre; and *Risky Business*—sleek, soulless, uncannily prescient, a cold-blooded indictment of the dawning Reagan era and a prototype for the rather more reactionary comedies of John Hughes. *Back to the Future,* in which time traveler Michael J. Fox must fend off the sexual advances of his horny teenaged mom to ensure that he will eventually be born, announces that the subgenre has entered its decadent phase.

Again, there is not much overlap between the Tale of Sexual Initiation and *Battle Royale*. Boy #16, Kazushi Niida, corners Girl #13, Takako Chigusa, and announces that he does not want to die a virgin; as an immediate consequence he dies a virgin. (And a gruesomely disfigured one at that.) The only girl who is presented in an overtly sexual fashion is #11, the predatory Mitsuko Souma, who racks up an impressive eight kills. The film implies that she seduces two of the boys before stabbing them to death; their nude corpses are visible on the ground as she dresses to leave.

In the novel and manga Mitsuko has an extensive and checkered sexual history, but the details are mostly omitted from the film. There is one flashback—included in the "Special Edition" but absent from the theatrical cut available on Netflix and elsewhere—in which Mitsuko's mother pimps her out to a john, and Mitsuko kills the john by shoving him down a flight of stairs. But again, the film is comparatively chaste, less interested in sex than in long-simmering adolescent crushes.

3. The John Hughes "Brat Pack" Movie. You know. *Sixteen Candles, Pretty in Pink, Weird Science, The Breakfast Club, Ferris Bueller's Day Off,* their various heirs and imitators. Audience-flattering comedies, alternately raucous and mawkish, about the quotidian tribulations of put-upon teens. Surely there can be no connection between—well, wait a minute. Put a pin in this one. We're coming back to it.

4. The High School Horror Show (incorporating the Teen Slasher Film). Jackpot. You'd have to have an ax in your skull to miss the similarities between *BR* and the enormously popular slasher subgenre, in which some long-buried trauma—the drowning of a child, the burning alive of a child-molesting janitor, the rejection of a homely, smelly fat guy who wants a pretty date for the Homecoming Dance—recrudesces, and a large cast of young, inexpensive performers begins to dwindle at the hands of an implacable, avenging, possibly supernatural force. The survivors, or "final girls," in Carol Clover's formulation, make it to the end credits by utilizing homicidal talents of their own.

Some of these teen-stalking monstrosities have distinct personalities (Freddy Krueger, of the *Nightmare on Elm Street* movies) while others are little more than masked ciphers (Michael Myers, *Halloween* and its sequels; Jason Voorhees, *Friday the 13th Pts.1–5, 271, 009.* Ghostface, of the semi-parodic *Scream* franchise, is a literal mask, worn by a variety of characters over the course of the series but always voiced by the same actor, Roger L. Jackson). The killers, however nondescript, always reappear in the sequels, often becoming pop-culture icons, but apart from Jamie Lee Curtis (*Halloween*) and Heather Langenkamp (*Nightmare*), the kids they stalk rarely return for later installments. The element of retribution therefore shrivels with each new outing: since the killers have long since taken their revenge upon the guilty, they must settle for whatever innocent victims are at hand. They no longer kill to avenge some forgotten sin; they just kill. You would almost think that audiences are not much concerned with morality or motivation and simply enjoy the spectacle of teenagers being slaughtered in inventive ways.

Is it wrong to say that *Battle Royale* simply eliminates the middleman?

One close spiritual antecedent of *Battle Royale* is almost, but not quite, a high school horror movie. In *Punishment Park* (1971), by the English director Peter Watkins, an unnamed president, presumably Richard Nixon, invokes the McCarron Act to round up any and all American citizens suspected of subversion. Antiwar activists, draft dodgers, black militants, radical feminists and protest singers are relocated to internment camps and paraded before tribunals composed of middle-aged Silent Majoritarians who are empowered to determine their fates without consideration of due process. The young dissidents tend to start out cool and sassy, expounding at great length upon the inequities and hypocrisies of American society, but are inevitably goaded into tantrums by the willful obtuseness of their accusers. When they begin to scream "FUCK YOU, PIGS," they are gagged, bound, and dragged from the courtroom for an extended Time Out.

At sentencing, each prisoner is offered a choice: a multi-year prison sentence, or . . . Punishment Park. Punishment Park is a barren fifty-mile stretch of desert in the American Southwest where midday temperatures reach 115 degrees. If the prisoners can cross the desert in three days, on foot, without food or water, and reach the American flag on the opposite side, they will be set free—or so they are told. Along the way they will have to elude capture by roving packs of state troopers and National Guardsmen in air-conditioned muscle cars, armed with live ammo and only too keen to test the dirty hippies' commitment to pacifism. Those who survive the hunt and reach the flag discover that what they have been telling us all along is true. The game is always rigged in favor of the house.

All this is framed in terms of intergenerational conflict. The young dissidents rant about institutional injustice, inequity, the need to change society, while their elders, who are perfectly content with the status quo, accuse them of ingratitude and personal irresponsibility ("Nobody made you blow up a building. You *chose* to be here"). Pinkos, radicals, and hippies are condemned to death because the daddy state is tired of hearing their sass. The politics of *Punishment Park,* steeped in late-sixties paranoia, are too ludicrous to be taken seriously—until one recalls that the movie is poised in time almost exactly midway between the Japanese-American internments of the Second World War and the post-Geneva horrors of Guantanamo Bay. Nowadays it's much harder to be ludicrous.

So what are the politics of *Battle Royale?* Early on we are told that the "BR Act" is a response to the economic collapse of Japan, a consequent epidemic of truancy and a rise in juvenile crime. But what social ill, specifically, is the BR Act meant to address? Does the practice of abducting children from school, dropping them on a deserted island, and forcing them to kill one another bolster consumer spending? Lower the crime rate? Discourage truancy?

Socially sanctioned battles-to-the-death are not uncommon in dystopian tales, but they usually have an explicit purpose—amusement of the decadent masses, say, or the avoidance of full-scale carnage. Tales of champion warfare, in which larger conflicts are settled by single combat, have been around since the *Iliad* (Hector vs. Achilles) and the Bible (David vs. Goliath). A famous science-fictional example is Fredric Brown's "Arena," in which a lone human must battle a lone alien to determine which species will survive; in the 1960s, the story was loosely adapted for television by both *The Outer Limits* and *Star Trek*. Peter Watkins' *The Gladiators* (1969), the immediate precursor to *Punishment Park,* is a variation on the premise, in which Cold War powers, hogtied by the inevitability of Mutual Assured Destruction, abandon their nuclear arsenals and agree to resolve their differences by proxy, sending crack combat teams into a high-tech arena to play a lethal game of (yes, again) capture the flag. Even the program of legalized murder in Elio Petri's *The 10th Victim* (1965) is designed to eliminate war, by providing an outlet for man's "natural urge to violence"; so we are told by the mustachioed emcee of the Sacher-Masoch Club, whose genial disquisition on the rules of the Big Hunt is wittily echoed by the *BR* orientation video with its chirpy schoolgirl narrator.

But the film shows absolutely no interest in the political underpinnings or societal consequences of the Program, and it's maddeningly inconsistent even on its own terms. In a prologue, the bloodied survivor of a previous contest emerges from a helicopter to breathless television coverage ("It's a girl!"), but the kids who arrive on the island seem blissfully unaware of both the games and the legislation that created them. From Kitano Sensei they receive a desultory explanation of the logic behind the program: "No good, that's what this country's become . . . Because of folks like Kuninobu here, this country is absolutely no good anymore. So the bigwigs got together and passed this law . . . Battle Royale!" The novel rationalizes the Program, unpersuasively, as a means of terrorizing the public into a mental state where rebellion is unthinkable, but even that pretext is beyond the scope of the film. A program that isn't publicized can have no deterrent value. Battle Royale is punishment, pure and simple. A roomful of ninth-graders must pay, unjustly, for the sins of others like them. It's as if someone has stolen Mr. Kitano's eraser, and the entire class will just have to fight to the death until the culprit 'fesses up.

It's arbitrary, whimsical, Kafkaesque. It's worse than algebra.

What do Japanese parents think about the BR Act? Do they accept the (dubious) necessity of having children plucked from their class-rooms and sent to their deaths? Do they complain? Do they resist? Do they ever attempt to intervene in the games? Do they train their toddlers in survival skills, knowing that a few years hence . . . ?

We don't know, because parents are, for the most part, conspicu-ously absent from Battle Royale. Apart from Mitsuko, the only student whose parent appears on-screen is our protagonist, Shuya Nanahara—"Boy 15." The first scene after the prologue establishes him as a proper receptacle for our sympathies. In flashback, Shuya comes home from school and discovers his widowed father dangling from an extension cord he has used as a makeshift noose. At his father's feet is a scroll containing not a suicide note, but messages of encouragement: "Go, Shuya! You can do it, Shuya!" The scroll is in fact a roll of toilet paper leading back to the bathroom, where Shuya promptly vomits.

The only adult authority figure is Kitano Sensei, standing in for the state. A year after being stabbed in the ass by a student, he has left teaching for more gratifying work as a BR administrator. In the first scene at the island he establishes his credentials as a disciplinarian by chucking a knife into one girl's head and detonating the explosive collar of Kuninobu, his would-be assailant. Later revelations bring his bona fides into question: he has an unwholesome fascination with Noriko, the one student who always appreciated him, and has created a little shrine to her, including a childlike painting in which she stands victorious over the bodies of her classmates. Noriko happens to have been the late Kuninobu's girlfriend.

In a deleted flashback, available on the Special Edition, Kitano explains his dilemma to Noriko over a popsicle. "The kids make fun of me at school . . . my own kid hates me. What do you think a grown-up should say to a kid now?" What he does say, to Shuya, is "Go, Shuya! You can do it, Shuya!"—the exact words of Shuya's dead father, a failure in life but a cheerleader to the end. In this case, however, the sensei is urging his student to pull a trigger and put him out of his misery. In the end he takes no more pleasure in murdering his students than he took in teaching them.

There are a few murderous teachers to be found in American high school horror films. For some reason, most of the real psychotics are coaches or gym teachers, like Dick Miller, the serial rapist of Jonathan Kaplan's *The Student Teachers* (1973), or Sally Kirkland in *Fatal Games* (1984), who has had to forfeit her Olympic medal—sex change; formerly male—and who takes out her frustrations by tossing a javelin at promising young athletes. The class of the group? Rock Hudson, in the truly mind-boggling Roger Vadim–Gene Roddenberry collaboration *Pretty Maids All in a Row* (1971), one of the *Ur*-texts of the slasher genre. Rock, when he is not coaching football, indulges his fondness for the voluptuous underage girls who populate every square foot of Oceanfront High, murdering them afterward to protect his reputation. Along the way he arranges for his virginal protégé, Ponce de Leon Harper, to have sex with hot teacher Angie Dickinson—see also: Tale of Sexual Initiation, The. *Pretty Maids* is, or was, as of last August, one of Quentin Tarantino's twelve favorite movies.

And where are the parents in the American Teen Horror Picture? As in Japan, they're elsewhere, mostly, because the exigencies of plot demand it. Teenagers naturally want to avoid the watchful eyes of their parents, so they sneak off to isolated venues where they can drink beer, make out, have sex—i.e., act like adults. In avoiding parental supervision, however, they forfeit parental protection, a dynamic that teen horror pictures have been quick to exploit since the fifties. Back then, the kids would start to neck in their borrowed car, and who would show up? The Blob. In the raunchier eighties, when horny teens find a vacant cot in an abandoned cabin and start ripping one another's clothes off, who's under the bed? Jason Voorhees, with a harpoon, ready to skewer a beast with two backs. Misbehave, and monsters appear!

Carol Clover's superb *Men, Women, and Chainsaws: Gender in the Modern Horror Film* (Princeton, NJ: Princeton University Press, 1992) dissects the process by which the sympathies of mostly male viewers shift from a voyeuristic stalker to a "final girl"—who is, as a rule, sexually chaste and slightly androgynous. But the cliches of the slasher cycle were well established and ripe for mockery by 1981, when *Student Bodies,* pseudonymously directed by Michael Ritchie, lampoons the standard have-sex-and-die/only-virgins-survive conventions of the subgenre (and coincidentally, introduces the running on-screen body count *BR* director Fukasaku would deploy, twenty years later, with a perfectly straight face).

You would almost think the various masked maniacs, the Jasons and Freddies and Leatherfaces, were acting *in loco parentis.* What are their machetes and cleavers but variations on the wagging parental finger? *I told you bad things would happen, but did you listen . . . ?* Or: *This is going to hurt you more than it hurts me.* But that story is so old it goes back to Genesis: the kids hang out with the wrong crowd, disobey the rules, eat of the Tree of Knowledge, and before you know it their angry paterfamilias has introduced them to Mortality. Freddie *et al* introduce the kids to mortality too, only sooner rather than later.

The film that deals most directly with parental influence is perhaps atypical of the genre, but is nonetheless credited with igniting the teen-horror boom of the late seventies/early eighties. It is also an unusually beautiful and moving example of the form. In Brian de Palma's *Carrie* (1976; from the novel by Stephen King), the fanatically religious Margaret White (Piper Laurie), confusing ignorance with innocence, has neglected to warn her teenage daughter about the onset of menses. The curse of Eve strikes at the most inconvenient moment—in the locker room—and Carrie (Sissy Spacek), who thinks she is bleeding to death, becomes a laughingstock to her classmates, who have already pigeonholed her as a weirdo because of her strict religious background and general air of naïveté.

A well-meaning teacher (Betty Buckley) undertakes the "normalization" of Carrie, which irritates the other girls even more and generates great tension in the White household. Worse yet, Carrie is cursed with psychic powers, and her emotional agitation manifests itself in eruptions of telekinesis. (She's repressed, all right—for good reason.) When Sue Snell (Amy Irving), the one genuinely kind girl in class, persuades her boyfriend to ask Carrie to the prom, Margaret forbids it, telling Carrie that she can never "fit in." But Carrie has by now begun to recognize both her mother's pathology and the extent of her own powers. For the first time she defies Mom.

Things do not work out well. The mean kids have conspired to elect Carrie prom queen, and at the moment of her crowning they empty a bucket of pig's blood onto her head. The horrified girl takes in the laughter of the crowd, realizes that Mom was right all along, and proceeds to slaughter everyone in the gym through pure force of will. Then she goes home, St.-Sebastians her mom with kitchen cutlery, and pulls the entire house down atop the two of them.

Sue Snell is the one survivor of the carnage, having been accidentally locked outside of the gym during Carrie's telekinetic rampage. In the dream sequence that ends the movie, she visits the ruins of Carrie's house, where a white cross (actually a "For Sale" sign) bears the hand-scrawled legend "Carrie White burns in Hell." As Sue lowers a bouquet of flowers to the gravesite, Carrie's bloody hand bursts upward from the rubble to grab her forearm. And there follows one of the most extraordinary cuts in movies, not as bold, perhaps, as the bone-to-satellite cut in *2001,* but at least as resonant: Sue White awakens in her own bed, screaming, with her mother clutching her forearm. We double-cut back to Carrie's hand, then again to Mrs.

Snell's to reinforce the connection. Camera pulls up and away from the bed as Sue's mother tries in vain to reassure her: "It's all right. I'm here. It's all right."

The last-minute jolt became a *de rigeur* feature of every horror film for the next quarter-century, but it camouflaged the real work the scene is doing. We see, in one quick stroke, Sue's responsibility for Carrie's death and the deaths of her classmates; Sue's "survivor guilt"; the (echoed) controlling hand of Carrie's mother, holding her back from the world; the (literal) controlling hand of Sue's mother, pulling her into a "safer" world where strangeness and difference and horror and guilt can all be successfully repressed. If Carrie is dragging Sue toward one type of grave, her mother is dragging her toward another.

Trust Mom, whom you cannot trust, whom you have no choice but to trust. It's the dilemma of every child, every adult. What do you think a grown-up should say to a kid now?

After a decade-plus of stalk 'n' slash, Carrie has metamorphosed into Veronica (Winona Ryder), the heroine of *Heathers* (dir. Michael Lehmann, 1988). Veronica is a wised-up girl, a tougher cookie than Carrie, but her school is a hot zone of status wars. She is not just bullied by the eponymous Heathers; she's bullied into bullying others as a condition of joining their clique. She falls under the influence of visionary bad-boy Jason "J.D." Dean (Christian Slater), who begins a program of targeted assassinations, enlisting Veronica as an initially unwitting accomplice. (She has a gift for forging suicide notes.) An epidemic of teen angst ensues, and eventually J.D.'s vision expands to include the destruction of the school and everyone in it. The culture of high school cannot be saved, only razed to the ground. As J.D. puts it in his famous dictum: "The only place different social types can genuinely get along is in heaven."

The film maintains its satirical verve for an hour or so, coasting on outrageousness (one girl attempts a copycat suicide out of a desire to be more popular), but the jokes become increasingly forced and sour toward the end as the filmmakers lose their nerve—or, if you prefer, come to their senses—and allow real-world morality to intrude upon what has so far been a hermetically tasteless universe. In Dan Waters's original script, Veronica kills J.D. before he can blow up the school, but then, in a nihilistic funk, straps the bomb around her own waist and detonates it. She winds up at a prom in heaven where all the warring factions do, in fact, get along famously, drinking blue Drano from a punchbowl. In the released film, Veronica thwarts the plot, looks on as J.D. immolates himself, and returns to school, announcing her intention to take over as "the new sheriff in town." Apparently she intends to preside over a kinder, gentler social hierarchy, because her first official act is to extend the hand of friendship to school pariah Martha Dunnstock, formerly known as "Martha Dumptruck." The scene reeks of phony sanctimony.

Heathers was made just in time. Fifteen years and a few real-life massacres later, the possibility of such bleak satire would all but vanish. The elegant, drifty camera of *Elephant* (dir. Gus van Sant, 2003) follows an assortment of high schoolers as they navigate the labyrinthine corridors of Watt H.S. in Portland, doubling back not only in space but in time as trivial incidents and casual encounters are replayed from different perspectives, simultaneously orienting and disorienting the viewer. The tracking shots recreate the experience of navigating through a first-person shooter, minus the soothing element of control. Murders are going to happen, but we don't know where, or when, or who will be the victims. There's little behavior, not much psychology, even less conventional "drama." There is no real suspense, only free-floating dread. Death is sudden, inevitable, and random all at once, a function of timing and geography. There's no pleasure to be extracted from the spectacle. There's no point in asking why it happened, what caused it, why one character died and another survived. You might as well ask why the universe insists on killing us all.

> *Do what thou wilt shall be the whole of the law.*
> —Aleister Crowley

Ferris Bueller (Matthew Broderick; *Ferris Bueller's Day Off*, 1986) is an affable teenaged sociopath who has the magical ability to get away with anything. He navigates the adult world effortlessly, because adult rules do not apply to him, and he always finds a convenient sap to take the fall for his shenanigans. When we meet him, he has convinced his parents he is too sick to go to school. His real plan is to spend the day knocking around Chicago, visiting the art museum, the stock exchange, a swank restaurant. For company, he arranges to have his girlfriend (Mia Sara) pulled out of class. For transportation, he calls on his hypochondriacal friend Cameron (Alan Ruck), whose father keeps a lovingly restored Ferrari in a glass-walled garage perched atop a woodsy hillside.

Ferris is worshipped by all his high school classmates; as assistant-to-the-principal Edie McClurg tells us, "Sportos, motorheads, geeks, sluts, spuds, wastoids, dweebies, and dickheads" all think he's a "righteous dude." His trickster cred is bottomless. The adults who dare to challenge his agenda meet with swift and merciless retribution. Woe betide the snooty, effeminate *maître d'* who offends Ferris's sense of entitlement when the boy hipster attempts to poach a reservation by posing as "Abe Froman, Sausage King of Chicago." A couple of slick moves later, Ferris & co. have assumed their rightful place at Abe's table, and the humiliated waiter is fawning over them. "It's understanding that makes it possible for people like us to tolerate a person like yourself," explains Ferris, oleaginously.

Despite its occasional detours into ugliness the picture zips along quite amiably, thanks to Broderick's affectless charm and a brilliant comic turn by Jeffrey Jones as the Wile E. Coyote principal whose efforts to entrap Ferris always backfire. Then, alas, it decides to reach for something more. Ferris's friend Cameron is troubled, full of doubt, held back from the level of true hipness to which he aspires—in other words, relegated to permanent sidekick status. By what? The opinion of others, specifically his father. He has borrowed the Ferrari and returned it without mishap, but he might yet be found out if his father checks the odometer. The car is up on blocks, running in reverse, when Cameron snaps. He begins to kick the car, smash at it. He knocks it off its blocks, and it hurtles backward through the glass wall, down the hillside, into the trees.

In a typical teen movie, the thematic oppositions would be clean and straightforward: Dad is materialistic and ignores his son, who commands attention by destroying the symbol of Dad's materialism. Here, though, the circumstances are rather more complicated. Cameron's dad does not appear in the picture. We do not actually see anything of his relationship with his son. All we are told is that he loves the Ferrari. But the materialist in this scenario is Ferris. Ferris has a computer, a swimming pool, an expensive sound system, and a synthesizer that generates coughing and wheezing noises at the touch of a key, but he complains, in an early scene, that his parents have not yet bought him a car. That is what makes him dependent on Cameron. Cameron hates catering to Ferris's whims, but he always submits, knowing that Ferris will eventually badger him into submission.

Ferris offers to take the blame when Dad finds out that the Ferrari is wrecked, but Cameron says no. He will accept the consequences of his symbolic gesture. "He'll be all right," Ferris tells his girlfriend, meaning that Cameron has lost his fear, that Ferris has finally taught him not to care what his dad thinks. The looming question, of course, is: when will he stop caring what Ferris thinks? As Ferris says, in another, slightly ironic context, "You can't respect someone who kisses your ass. It just doesn't work."

The hugely successful eighties comedies of John Hughes embody, or at least cater to, a distinctly teenage mindset. His characters are marked by A) a deep-seated aversion to parental authority, and B) a carefully nurtured resentment of parental neglect, contradictory qualities which coexist without apparent friction in the teenage brain. Some of his best plots are set in motion by a shocking act of parental malfeasance. In *Sixteen Candles* (1984), Molly Ringwald's parents are so preoccupied with the preparations for her sister's wedding that they completely forget Molly's sixteenth birthday. In *Home Alone* (dir. Chris Columbus, 1990), the extremely fecund McCallisters have so many kids to wrangle on their holiday trip to Paris that they accidentally leave one behind. Young Kevin (Macaulay Culkin) initially enjoys staying up late, bouncing on beds, lip-syncing in the mirror, etc., until a pair of cartoonish burglars invade the house and unleash his inner psychopath. What follows is not unlike a slasher pic in which the same victims die over and over, but somehow keep coming back for more. Did I mention that Hughes's first major writing credit was on *National Lampoon's Class Reunion* (1982), a slasher parody set at Lizzie Borden High School?

With a few exceptions—there are plenty of indications, e.g., that Ferris Bueller is a monster, albeit a likeable one—the films do not invite much self-reflection. They mostly corroborate the teenage worldview: *Adults do not understand us. We deserve better from adults.* In a few cases they openly pander to the adolescent sense of self-importance: "Don't You Forget About Me," the bombastic synth-pop *cri de coeur* that plays under the credits of *The Breakfast Club* (1985)—and that is referenced as a classic in the 2012 college comedy *Pitch Perfect*—is probably the second funniest thing in the movie. First place goes to the epigraph, from David Bowie's "Changes." You know the one—about the children being spit on "as they try to change their world."

The Breakfast Club is in some ways the flip side of *Battle Royale.* Five kids, guilty of various petty offenses, are forced to serve Saturday detention (!) under the supervision of a teacher who proves, unsurprisingly, to be venal, dishonest, and domineering. There's a Jock (Emilio Estevez), a Nerd (Anthony Michael Hall), a Princess (Molly Ringwald), a Criminal (Judd Nelson), and a "Basket Case" (Ally Sheedy)—although all five resent being stereotyped as such. (By whom? The film's publicists?) Their initial bickering evolves into an impromptu encounter-group session, in which it transpires that they are not mere stereotypes, but Stereotypes with Excuses: the criminal has been abused by his alcoholic father, the jock driven to earn a wrestling scholarship by his financially strapped parents, etc. Eventually they unite in defiance of the teacher's authority. By breaking out of the library, smoking dope, dancing, and pairing off, they develop a common bond and a new social order. The artistic girl, the "basket case," who is introduced simulating a snowfall by combing her dandruff onto a picture of a covered bridge, discovers that with a few hair and makeup tips, she can win the attentions of the wrestler. The prom queen discovers that she secretly kinda likes it when the criminal pushes her around and talks dirty to her, because he must have a heart of gold in there somewhere, if you want to blast for it. The nerd discovers that nerds don't get girls.

Meet the new world, same as the old world. Hughes's characters cannot really envision a serious alternative to the social structures their parents have bequeathed them. Do they really want to change the world? Or do they just want adults to get out of the way and give them the run of it—which is what *always* happens, sooner or later?

In *Battle Royale,* as he's making his escape from the island with Noriko and Shogo, Shuya says, "I've never trusted grown-ups—my dad and my mom ran off or died 'cause they felt like it. But I'll keep fighting . . . until I become a real adult."

At the opening of *Battle Royale II: Requiem,* we learn that Shuya has postponed that transition. In fact, his distaste for the grown-up world is more virulent than ever. After demolishing a series of skyscrapers in a Japanese metropolis (a pair of disturbingly familiar twin towers are the first to go), Shuya and his terrorist group, "Wild Seven," take to the airwaves to claim credit for the atrocity. They will never forgive those who "made us murder each other" in the earlier film. "Let us now declare war against every last adult!"

It's a Hughesian sentiment, although no Hughes kid would express it in so blunt a fashion. One must wonder what sort of consensus the Terrorist would have forged with the Jock, the Nerd, the Princess, the Criminal, and the Basket Case.

But, by the same token, one must wonder how the members of the Breakfast Club would have fared in a battle royale. Imagine the five of them in mortal combat. For that matter, imagine Kevin McCallister, building booby traps in the trees. Imagine the snakelike Ferris Bueller, charming victims into his clutches.

Go ahead, imagine it. Isn't that why you bought the ticket?

LOGLINE: *In the near future, an authoritarian government air-lifts the entire population of Hollywood High onto a deserted island and forces them to fight to the death. Finally.*

Ferris Bueller has sex with Laurie Strode (Jamie Lee Curtis; *Halloween,* 1978). Mere seconds later she is slain by a masked, knife-wielding maniac who jumps out from behind a bush.

The Jock, the Princess, the Criminal, and the Basket Case decide, in lieu of killing each other, to explore their commonalities by dancing to British synth-pop (Simple Minds, OMD, the Psychedelic Furs, etc.) on a bluff overlooking the water. Riff Randell (P.J. Soles; *Rock 'n' Roll High School,* 1979) arrives, pops her Ramones mix tape into the cassette deck and cranks the volume up to 11. The song "Cretin Hop" generates intense seismic vibrations, causing a large section of cliff to break free and fall into the ocean, taking most of the partiers with it. Riff is pogoing so vigorously that she does not notice their absence until three Heathers (Shannen Doherty, Lisanne Falk, Kim Walker; *Heathers,* 1988) appear, demanding that she "turn down that awful fucking noise." When she refuses, the Heathers attack her speakers with croquet mallets. Riff retaliates by detonating a nearby fertilizer truck, partly out of spite toward the Heathers, partly because she has always wondered how it would feel to be blown up by a fertilizer truck.

Ferris Bueller has sex with Nancy Thompson (Heather Langenkamp; *Nightmare on Elm Street,* 1981). Mere seconds later she is slain by a scarred, steel-clawed maniac who jumps out from behind a bush.

Thrift-store ragamuffin Andie Walsh (Molly Ringwald; *Pretty in Pink,* 1986), while wandering the beach down below, finds "Princess" Claire Standish's clothes, her makeup case, and her stash of *Teen Glamor* magazines. Before you can say "makeover" she's the spitting image of Claire. Phil "Duckie" Dale (Jon Cryer) has always longed to kill Andie, but he realizes that in her cleaned-up state she can attract a richer, better-looking killer, such as classy WASP dreamboat Blane McDonough (Andrew McCarthy). The selfless Duckie allows Blane to strangle Andie in the parking lot, knowing that she will die happy, and settles for killing Blane afterward.

Gary Wallace (Anthony Michael Hall) and Wyatt Donnelly (Ilan-Mitchell Smith; *Weird Science,* 1985) discover a computer equipped with a scanner. By inputting a muscle magazine, a Frank Frazetta cover illustration, and a VHS tape of two *Outer Limits* episodes, they magically summon up the Terminator (Arnold Schwarzenegger; *The Terminator,* 1984) to protect them from the depredations of brother Chip (Bill Paxton) and his cronies from military school, Brian Moreland (Tim Hutton), Alec Dwyer (Sean Penn), and David Shawn (Tom Cruise; *Taps,* 1981). The cadets attempt to forestall doom by complimenting the Teutonic automaton on his impressive ordnance, his well-oiled biceps, etc., but to no avail. The Terminator's advanced facial-recognition software has already identified David Shawn as the young man who will survive the battle, go to law school, enter the public sector, and successfully prosecute the board of Enron. He therefore massacres David and the rest of the group, including the nerds, in a show of loyalty to his corporate makers. Only Dwyer escapes, by switching outfits with an amiable lookalike stoner, Jeff Spicoli (Sean Penn; *Fast Times at Ridgemont High,* 1982), who has earlier made the mistake of offering him a joint.

Danny Zuko (John Travolta), Sandy Olsen (Olivia Newton-John), and Betty Rizzo (Stockard Channing; *Grease,* 1978) die of old age before the other "kids" get a crack at them.

The suave teenage drug dealer played by Charlie Sheen in *Ferris Bueller's Day Off* eludes extermination by pimping his crack ho, Jeannie Bueller (Jennifer Grey), out to the male contestants. However, when she categorically refuses to do Duckie Dale, he strangles her in a fit of pique. Now lacking his "insurance policy," he kills Alec Dwyer for Spicoli's stash of weed, which he plans to disseminate widely to his rivals, "mellowing them out" for the kill. But first, in a gesture of solidarity, he fires up a joint with Duckie, and the two quickly discover that, despite their ostensibly discordant personalities, they complement each other quite nicely. They are discussing the possibility of rearing a son together when one of them steps on a tripwire, and a section of tree trunk swings down from above, pulverizing both their skulls. Early-admission student Kevin McCallister clambers down from the tree and begins planning his next booby trap.

Ferris Bueller has sex with Sally Hardesty (Marilyn Burns; *The Texas Chain Saw Massacre,* 1974). Mere moments later she is slain by a masked, chain saw-wielding maniac who jumps out from behind a bush.

Seventy years in the future, Morty McFly (Michael J. Fox), the middle-aged grandson of Marty McFly (Michael J. Fox; *Back to the Future,* 1985), realizes that the Terminator's appearance on the island has altered the past, and jumps into his time-traveling DeLorean jetcar to undo the damage. In the old timeline, Marty won the battle royale. In the new, revised timeline, Marty is killed by Joel Goodsen (Tom Cruise; *Risky Business,* 1983), who will go on to attend Harvard Law, enter the public sector, and successfully prosecute the board of Enron. Unless he can somehow save Marty, Morty will never be born. Alas, just as Morty is arriving in the past, his jetcar collides with the Terminator, who is on his way back to the future, and the wreckage lands on Marty, killing him instantly. As a result, Morty is never born—but how, then, does he crash into the Terminator? The ensuing paradox storm ravages multiple quantum universes, none of which should concern us here.

Veronica and J.D. (*Heathers*) are on their way to the observation post of the abandoned lighthouse, where they plan to keep an eye on the other contestants and make fun of the handicapped. At the top of the spiral staircase, however, J.D. steps on a tripwire, emptying a bucket of ball bearings onto the steps. Kevin McCallister cackles with glee as the two of them tumble ass over teakettle down the stairs, landing, finally, at the heavenly prom.

Unfortunately for Kevin, Carrie White is watching all this from the shore, and jokes involving buckets make Carrie see red. Parts of Kevin's body are eventually discovered in Waco, Texas; Laguna Beach; and Saskatchewan.

Katniss Everdeen (Jennifer Lawrence; *The Hunger Games*, 2012) realizes she is on the wrong damned island. She phones the studio, which immediately sends a boat to fetch her. As she's leaving she spies Joel Goodsen (Tom Cruise; *Risky Business*, 1983) lip-syncing to "My Ding-a-Ling" and shoots an arrow into his back, just to stay in practice.

Carrie sees Ferris Bueller, thinks about having sex with him, and explodes.

Ferris Bueller has sex with his girlfriend, Sloane. He waits and waits, but this time Cameron refuses to jump out from behind the bush. Disgusted, Ferris proposes marriage to Sloane. When she puckers up to kiss him, he pulls a nail file from her purse and lets her have it between the ribs.

Just then, Joel Goodsen stumbles out of the woods with Katniss's arrow still quivering in his back. He knows he's a goner but has sworn nonetheless to kill Ferris for swiping his stolen-Porsche gag, and for topping his lip-sync gag. With his final breath he opens fire on Ferris. Ferris gestures to Cameron, who immediately flings himself into the path of the bullets.

Ferris kneels beside his fallen friend and cradles his head. "You shouldn't have done that," he says.

Cameron opens his eyes. "I didn't," he replies, at which point Ferris realizes that Cameron is wearing a bulletproof vest. Worse yet, he has somehow managed to put his mitts on Sloane's nail file. While Ferris is cooking up a clever subterfuge, Cameron slits his throat.

Cameron is declared the winner. A helicopter descends to fetch him. Back home, he tells the TV crews: "I'll never forget this day. This was the best day of my life. I survived."

ENDNOTES

1 Quoted in Akiko Fujita, 'The Hunger Games,' a Japanese Original? ABC News. March 22, 2012. (online) http://abcnews.go.com/blogs/headlines/2012/03/the-hunger-games-a-japanese-original/

Whatever You Encounter, Slay It at Once: *Battle Royale* as Zen Parable

BY DOUGLAS F. WARRICK

The teachings of Linji Yixuan remain a cornerstone of Zen Buddhist philosophy more than 1,100 years after his death. The centerpiece of Linji's teachings is the concept of the true man without rank. Linji describes the true man thusly:

> The master, taking the high seat in the hall, said, "On your lump of red flesh is a true man without rank who is always going in and out of the face of every one of you. Those who have not yet confirmed this, look, look!"[1]

Linji rarely makes explicit the parameters that define the True Man's behavior. He instead seeks to dissolve his students' culturally inherited ideas of rank through absurdity, provocation, and violence. The True Man is an ideal toward which students are meant to aspire, a person who has woken up to their enlightenment by removing themselves from the false dichotomies of social hierarchy. That is to say, the True Man of No Rank is neither at the top of the totem pole, nor at its bottom, nor anywhere in between. He or she has transcended the entire idea of rank and authority.

Kinji Fukasaku's film adaptation of *Battle Royale* is at its core a film about rejecting authority. Noriko, Shuya, and their classmates are constantly faced with the social consequences of hierarchy, from the obvious expectations placed upon them by their educators (in particular, their homeroom teacher, the quietly menacing Kitano) and their government to the more pernicious hierarchies imposed by gender roles and the nebulous regulations of adolescent "cool." The only reason they survive is that they are able to reject and transcend these hierarchies rather than attempting to climb them. In that sense, Noriko and Shuya are illustrative of the ideal Zen students, and their survival serves as a stand-in for Zen enlightenment.

In *The Record of Linji*, the master places repeated emphasis on the supposed authority of typically revered figures and the importance of rejecting that authority. One famous koan attributed to Linji goes like this:

> Followers of the Way, if you want insight into dharma as it is, just don't be taken in by the deluded views of others. Whatever you encounter, either within or without, slay it at once. On meeting a buddha slay the buddha, on meeting a patriarch slay the patriarch, on meeting an arhat slay the arhat, on meeting your parents slay your parents, on meeting your kinsman slay your kinsman, and you attain emancipation. By not cleaving to things, you freely pass through. [2]

In Linji's koan, the word "slay" acts as useful shorthand for the more complex process of philosophical rejection, and it's able to serve this purpose precisely because of society's edict against murder. But in *Battle Royale*, murder has been institutionalized as a means by which the state maintains hierarchical authority. The BR Initiative reinforces the artificial authority of military and educational figures by taking a disenfranchised population and turning its rage against itself. In that sense, violence becomes an act of reinforcement rather than one of rebellion, and death becomes the ultimate form of submission to authority.

It's no wonder, then, that the students most willing to conform to Kitano's expectations are also doomed to fail. It's notable that the first student in the film who follows orders and kills a classmate, the sweaty and terrified Akamatsu, is himself killed almost immediately thereafter.

Akamatsu's death sets a precedent. Again and again, the members of Class B follow the rules set by authority figures, turn their alienation against one another, and are rewarded for their obedience with swift and often nasty deaths. Oki attacks Shuya and ends up splitting his own cranium with the ax he was issued at the beginning of the game. Before he's gunned down, Motobuchi explicitly states that he intends to win so that he can meet cultural expectations by one day getting into a prestigious university. The lighthouse crew self-destructs when Sakaki attempts to poison Shuya's food and feeds it instead to Yuka, sparking the exact sort of distrust and infighting the BR program is designed to provoke.

In all of these cases, the students trust the word of a corrupt government and a sadistic teacher over themselves and their peers. They take the word of their betters as sacred without really understanding why. Linji warns against delineating "sacred" sources from more mundane ones. "If you love the sacred and hate the secular, you'll float and sink in the sea of birth-and-death."[3]

The overt authority of the government isn't the only force exerting itself over the students. They are punished just as severely for submitting to more pernicious hierarchies, especially those associated with the adolescent social structure. Early in the film, a group of students led by Numai confront the psychotic "transfer student" Kiriyama, accusing him (quite rightly) of being in league with Kitano and the military. Numai's gang believes that they can stop the game if they neutralize Kiriyama. That seems to be a noble sentiment, but the way they express it is by engaging in the same sort of petty bullying commonly used by high schoolers to ostracize those outside their social circle. They slap him in the head with a fan, push him around, toy with him like he's the uncool pretender to their cool-kid clique, and each and every one of them dies for their trouble. They may have rebelled against the letter of the BR law, but by participating in the hierarchy of coolness, they've obeyed it in spirit.

The irony, of course, is that Kiriyama may be the coolest character in the film. With his slim black suit, his casual sneakers, his colorful hair, his sneering silence, Kiriyama is every inch the rock star, a comic book character come to life. His relative success is intrinsically tied to his ability to intimidate the competition into reacting to the iconography of cool that he employs. Even Shinji and his hacker buddies, who make the most direct insurrectionist overtures against Kitano with their computer virus and their bomb-building, are ultimately brought down by the surreally hip Kiriyama. He's not the only character in the film who utilizes that tactic fruitfully, either.

Mitsuko Souma's ruthlessness and manipulation call to mind the archetypal high school mean girl. When she finds Megumi hiding in the shed, she wins her trust ("I was never friendly with your clique," says the hapless and lovesick Megumi, "but you're okay.") before humiliating and murdering her. She plays the hysterical and perse-cuted victim when confronted by Hirono and accused of stealing her boyfriend and then drops the act immediately when she gains the upper hand. Intriguingly, the film hints that Mitsuko may have been less queen bee than outcast prior to the events of the film. Her classmates refer to her by her given name instead of more respectfully using her surname. She screams, "Why does everybody gang up on me?" when confronted by Hirono. In voice-over, just before she dies, Mitsuko says, "I just didn't want to be a loser anymore." If indeed these clues hint at a history as a high school outcast, Mitsuko games the system by redefining her place in the hierarchy, by casting herself as the highest ranking figure instead of as one of the lowest. It works, for a while. Ultimately, however, her reliance and faith in that system of hierarchy fails her when she comes up against Kiriyama, someone whose reliance on coolness is more tactical than hers.

So, when Linji's "slaying" metaphor has been coopted and cor-rupted by the very people he advocates slaying, how does a good Zen student break the cycle? The only way to win is not to play.

The first students who take a stand against the dictums of the BR Act are Yamamoto and Ogawa. "I know one thing," says Ogawa before throwing herself off a cliff, "I'll never play this game." Still, even while they reject BR, they accept the rank they've been assigned. "Can't anyone help us?" asks Yamamoto, to which Ogawa replies, "Nobody can." The only salvation of which they can conceive is that granted by outside agents, and as such, they fail to achieve the enlightenment to which survival is analogous. As Linji said, "Followers of the Way, your own present activities do not differ from those of the patriarch-buddhas. You just don't believe this and keep on seeking outside."[4]

One of the most interesting scenes in the film, the confrontation between Chigusa and Niida, is a reversal of the scene between Yamamoto and Ogawa. Whereas Yamamoto and Ogawa reject the game but comply with societal expectations, Chigusa claims to have every intention of winning the battle royale and won't allow the pressures of systemic misogyny to get in her way. Niida is a textbook product of rape culture. Over the course of two minutes, he pinballs between trying to manipulate Chigusa emotionally ("They all gossiped about us . . . you liked it," "I'm in love with you," "We're gonna die anyway. Don't you want to do it once before you die?") and threatening her with violence if she doesn't sleep with him ("Run and I shoot," "I've already killed. I could force you to do it now," "It's your fault, you made me mad"). Chigusa kills Niida, stabbing him in the crotch and symbolically rejecting the dominant paradigm that expects women to submit to the sexual will of men.

But of course, Chigusa also dies. So what's the secret? How are Shuya and Noriko any different from Chigusa or Yamamoto or Ogawa? No matter whether the hierarchy to which they are subjected is official or customary, they reject it. Whereas Numai's gang reacts to Kiriyama with customary high school nastiness, Shuya and Noriko react to Kawada (Kiriyama's good-guy counterpart, another "transfer student" whose status as an outsider serves the same purpose) initially with quiet distrust and eventually with acceptance. Rather than working within the system to find transcendence, as Kiriyama and Mitsuko do, they seek to remove themselves from the system entirely by finding a way off the island.

Noriko even shows some degree of compassion for Kitano, the most reviled man on the island. "I had a dream," she says. "I was alone with Kitano on an empty riverbank . . . But Kitano seemed lonely." Later, when Kitano tries to goad Noriko into shooting him, she denies him. In so doing, Noriko manages to defy her teacher's final attempt to exert control over her. By humanizing Kitano, Noriko not only rejects Kitano's authority, but rejects the entire idea of authority. She transcends rank by equalizing herself and Kitano, in much the same way that Linji encourages his students to reject his own authority. Many passages from *The Record of Linji* depict the master encouraging his students to reject his own supposed authority. He demands that students answer their own koans, strikes them with his whisk when they bow to him, and in the following passage, rewards a student for removing him from a physical place of prominence:

> One day Linji went to He Prefecture. The governor, Councilor Wang, requested the master to take the high seat.
>
> At that time Mayu came forward and asked, "The Great Compassionate One has a thousand hands and a thousand eyes. Which is the true eye?"
>
> The master said, "The Great Compassionate One has a thousand hands and a thousand eyes. Which is the true eye? Speak, speak!"
>
> Mayu pulled the master down off the high seat and sat on it himself.
>
> Coming up to him, the master said, "How do you do?"
> Mayu hesitated.
>
> The master, in his turn, pulled Mayu down off the high seat and sat upon it himself. Mayu went out. The master stepped down.[5]

Linji wants his students to reject all authority, including his and even their own. By showing Mayu respect after being dethroned, Linji rewards him. But when Mayu hesitates, he's reverting back to the old power structures. So it's Linji's turn to challenge Mayu's rank.

The connection between Linji—the master who teaches his students to reject his rank as well as their own—and Kitano—the antagonist who appears to advocate for deference to authority—deserves exploration. When the film begins, Kitano appears to sympathize with the rationale behind the BR Act. He berates the students for being disrespectful, for boycotting school, for mistrusting adults. But if Kitano serves only to represent the fascistic zeal of the authoritarian class, what should we make of his disdain for the military personnel with whom he's ostensibly colluding? What should be made of the loneliness Noriko perceives in him and the phone calls he receives from his daughter? He uses a squirt gun to threaten Noriko at the film's climax, even though he has an actual gun in his possession. Why would he use a toy gun if he didn't want the power and control he exerts to be subverted and transcended?

Kitano recognizes that he is a dinosaur, that he's outlived his usefulness. He goes out of his way to orchestrate his own destruction at the hands of those whose rank is below his own. His squirt gun is Linji's whisk, a different form of the same tool, a means by which to shock young monks into rejecting the duality of the student-mentor relationship. Whether he intends to be or not, Kitano becomes the film's Zen master, guiding his students toward enlightenment through confrontation, absurdity, and subversion.

By the end of the film, he seems to have accomplished that purpose. When we see Shuya and Noriko emerge from the Shibuya subway station, they've transcended not only the student-mentor duality, but the entire body of dualisms that ties a person to the culture into which they are born. They exist apart from society. They are without rank, rejecters of home both literally and intellectually. *The Record of Linji* has much to say on the subject of homes. Any idea outside of oneself is seen as a home in which one hides. Those who trade one authority for another "have only left one house to enter another."[6] But those who abandon the safety of allowing themselves to be defined by others understand that "no real dharma exists. Those who understand this are true renouncers of home, and may spend a million gold coins a day."[7]

Or as Shuya puts it, "No matter how far, run for all you're worth."

ENDNOTES

1. Ruth Fuller Sasaki, trans., *The Record of Linji* (Hawaii: University of Hawaii Press, 2009), 4.
2. Sasaki, *The Record of Linji*, 22.
3. Sasaki, *The Record of Linji*, 12.
4. Sasaki, *The Record of Linji*, 22.
5. Sasaki, *The Record of Linji*, 4.
6. Sasaki, *The Record of Linji*, 12.
7. Sasaki, *The Record of Linji*, 13.

About the Contributors

Nadia Bulkin writes scary stories about the scary world we live in. Her fiction has appeared in *ChiZine, Creatures: Thirty Years of Monsters, Fantasy Magazine,* and *Strange Horizons,* among others. She lives in Washington, D.C., works in policy, and tends her garden of student debt sowed by two political science degrees. For more, see nadiabulkin.wordpress.com.

Carrie Cuinn is an author, editor, bibliophile, modernist, and geek. In her spare time she listens to music, watches indie films, cooks everything, reads voraciously, publishes a magazine, and sometimes gets enough sleep. You can find her online at @CarrieCuinn or at http://carriecuinn.com.

Raechel Dumas is a doctoral student in Japanese residing in Boulder, Colorado.

Toh EnJoe was born in Hokkaido in 1972. After completing a PhD at the University of Tokyo, he became a researcher in theoretical physics. In 2007 he won the Bungakukai Shinjinsho (Literary World Newcomer's) Prize with "Of the Baseball." That same year brought the publication of his book *Self-Reference ENGINE,* which caused a sensation in SF circles and was ranked No. 2 on *SF Magazine*'s list of the best science fiction of the year. Since then, EnJoe has been one of those rare writers comfortable working in both "pure literature" and science fiction. In 2010 his novel *U Yu Shi Tan* won the Noma Prize for new authors. In 2011 his "This Is a Pen" was nominated for the Akutagawa Prize, and he won Waseda University's Tsubouchi Shouyou Prize. In January 2012, he won the Akutagawa Prize with "Doukeshi no Cyo" (*Harlequin's Butterflies*). His other works include *Boy's Surface, About Goto,* and his latest novel *Empire of Corpses* (cowritten with the late Project Itoh).

Isamu Fukui was born in New York City to a Japanese father and a Korean mother. A distaste for school inspired him to pen his first novel, *Truancy,* at the age of fifteen. His latest novel, *Truancy City,* was published in 2012 and completes a trilogy about the tyranny of compulsory education. He graduated from New York University in the same year and found it much more agreeable than high school.

Failed cartoonist Sam Hamm turned to screenwriting when he realized he would never be able to draw like Alex Toth. His feature credits include *Never Cry Wolf, Batman, Batman Returns,* and *Monkeybone.* Hamm also created the short-lived television series *M.A.N.T.I.S.* in collaboration with Sam Raimi. His script for "Homecoming," directed by Joe Dante for the Showtime series *Masters of Horror,* won a Best Screenplay award at the Sitges International Film Festival. Although he still cannot draw like Alex Toth, Hamm did eventually get to write Batman's fiftieth anniversary adventure, "Blind Justice," for DC Comics.

Masao Higashi is an anthologist, literary critic, and editor of the magazine *Yū* (Ghosts), which specializes in Kwaidan, the traditional ghost stories of Japan. He is the editor of *Sekai Gensō Bungaku Taizen* (Global Encyclopedia of Fantasy Literature), *Kaiki: Uncanny Tales from Japan* (Kurodahan Press, English language), and several collections of ghost stories and critical works. In 2011 he won the 64th Mystery Writers of Japan Prize for his work *Tōno Monogatari* (Tales of Distant Fields).

Brian Keene writes novels, comic books, short fiction, and occasional journalism for money. He is the author of over forty books, mostly in the horror, crime, and dark fantasy genres. His 2003 novel, *The Rising,* is often credited (along with Robert Kirkman's *The Walking Dead* comic and Danny Boyle's film *28 Days Later*) with inspiring pop culture's current interest in zombies. Keene's novels have been translated into German, Spanish, Polish, Italian, French, and many more. In addition to his own original work, Keene has written for media properties such as *Doctor Who, Hellboy, Masters of the Universe,* and *Superman.* Several of Keene's novels have been developed for film, including *Ghoul, The Ties That Bind,* and *Fast Zombies Suck.* Several more are in development or under option. Keene's work has been praised in such diverse places as the *New York Times,* The History Channel, *The Howard Stern Show,* CNN.com, *Publisher's Weekly,* Media Bistro, *Fangoria Magazine,* and *Rue Morgue Magazine.* He has won numerous awards and honors, including two Bram Stoker Awards and a recognition from Whiteman A.F.B. (home of the B-2 Stealth Bomber) for his outreach to US troops serving both overseas and abroad. A prolific public speaker, Keene has delivered talks at conventions, college campuses, theaters, and inside Central Intelligence Agency headquarters in Langley, VA.

Gregory Lamberson is the author of the occult detective series The Jake Helman Files, as well as the werewolf series The Frenzy Cycle and the first TREEbook (Timed Reading Experience E-book), *The Julian Year.* He is also a filmmaker, responsible for the eighties' cult film *Slime City,* its sequel *Slime City Massacre,* and *Dry Bones.* His website is www.gregorylamberson.com.

Kathleen Miller spent her formative years in Gilroy, CA, before attending UC Berkeley, where she wrote her honors thesis on Ray

Bradbury and the pathology of authorship. She is still trying to lure her own inner child into her unmarked van with promises of sugary treats. In her spare time, she masquerades on Twitter as @the_amazing_kat, and is currently working on a children's book about the adventures of a bioluminescent cat, its mad scientist human, and his robotic creation: the RoboCat5000™.

Konstantine Paradias is a jeweler by profession and a writer by choice. His short stories have been published in Third FlatIron's *Lost Worlds* anthology, *Unidentified Funny Objects! 2,* and the LeoDeGrance.com flash fiction anthology. People tell him he has a writing problem, but he says he can quit, like, whenever he wants. You can find him on FaceBook (https://www.facebook.com/konstantine.paradias) or follow him on Twitter (@KostantineP) or you can cut the middle man and go straight for his blog, Shapescapes (http://shapescapes.blogspot.com).

Jason S. Ridler is a writer and historian. He is the author of the vampire-fight-club novel *A Triumph for Sakura* and the MMA noir *Blood and Sawdust.* He has published over sixty short stories in such magazines and anthologies as *The Big Click, Beneath Ceaseless Skies,* and *Out of the Gutter.* A former punk rock musician and cemetery groundskeeper, Jason holds a PhD in War Studies from the Royal Military College of Canada.

Adam Roberts is a British writer and university professor. He is the author of fourteen novels, the most recent of which are *Jack Glass* (Gollancz, 2012) and *Twenty Trillion Leagues Under the Sea* (Gollancz, 2014). He has published various academic studies of SF and fantasy, as well as nineteenth-century literature and culture. He is married with two children and lives a little way west of London, an English town.

John Skipp is the only *New York Times* best-selling novelist to win a pornographic Oscar for a scene with a singing penis. His splatterpunk novel *The Light at the End* inspired the character of Spike from *Buffy the Vampire Slayer.* His 1989 anthology *Book of the Dead* was the beginning of modern post-Romero zombie fiction. His short fiction with Cody Goodfellow has graced *Hellboy: Oddest Jobs* and the latest *Zombies vs. Robots* collection. Their latest book is *The Last Goddamn Hollywood Movie.* Skipp is also the editor of four massive, encyclopedic anthologies (*Zombies, Demons, Psychos, Werewolves & Shapeshifters*), and editor-in-chief of mainstream-meets-Bizarro publishing imprint Fungasm Press. And as filmmaker, he and Andrew Kasch have co-directed the award-winning lactating manboob horror comedy *Stay at Home Dad* and the Slow Poisoner music video *Hot Rod Worm,* with Robot Chicken stop motion animator Michael Granberry, in which Skipp also plays the bongos. He lives in L.A.

Steven R. Stewart grew up listening to his dad's ghost stories and never recovered. His short fiction has appeared in *Drabblecast, Redstone, Intergalactic Medicine Show* and others; his nonfiction has been featured by Science Fiction and Fantasy Writers of America.

Douglas F. Warrick is an American writer living in Daegu, South Korea. His first collection of short stories, *Plow the Bones,* is available from Apex Publications. You can visit him online at www.douglasfwarrick.com.

Copyright Acknowledgments

BATTLE ROYALE
ANGELS' BORDER

STORY BY KOUSHUN TAKAMI // ART BY MIOKO OHNISHI & YOUHEI OGUMA

A *BATTLE ROYALE* MANGA

FINALLY, DISCOVER THE POIGNANT, TRAGIC STORY OF THE GIRLS IN THE LIGHTHOUSE.

HARUKA TANIZAWA IS AN AVERAGE JUNIOR HIGH STUDENT. SHE PLAYS ON THE VOLLEYBALL TEAM AND JUST FELL IN LOVE FOR THE FIRST TIME. BUT HER LOVE IS ALSO HER BEST FRIEND AND CLASSMATE, YUKIE, AND HARUKA DREADS THE TRUTH COMING OUT AND RUINING THEIR RELATIONSHIP.

AND THEN HER ENTIRE CLASS IS DRUGGED, DRAGGED TO A DESERTED ISLAND AND FORCED TO PARTICIPATE IN THE BLOODY SPECTACLE OF THE PROGRAM.

WHILE MOST OF THE STUDENTS SCATTER AS SOON AS THEY'RE RELEASED FROM THE STAGING GROUNDS, YUKIE COMES BACK FOR HARUKA, AND TOGETHER THEY GATHER SOME OF THE OTHER GIRLS IN THE DUBIOUS SAFETY OF THE ISLAND'S LIGHTHOUSE.

THEY KNOW SURVIVAL IS UNLIKELY.
BUT WHAT ABOUT HOPE...?

$12.99USA // $14.99CAN // £8.99UK | 5.75"x8.25" | ISBN: 978-1-4215-7168-3

HAIKASORU
THE FUTURE IS JAPANESE

SELF-REFERENCE ENGINE BY TOH ENJOE

This is not a novel.

This is not a short story collection.

This is Self-Reference ENGINE.

Instructions for Use: Read chapters in order. Contemplate the dreams of twenty-two dead Freuds. Note your position in spacetime at all times (and spaces). Keep an eye out for a talking bobby sock named Bobby Socks. Beware the star-man Alpha Centauri. Remember that the chapter entitled "Japanese" is translated from the Japanese, but should be read in Japanese. Warning: if reading this book on the back of a catfish statue, the text may vanish at any moment, and you may forget that it ever existed.

From the mind of Toh EnJoe comes Self-Reference ENGINE, a textual machine that combines the rigor of Stanislaw Lem with the imagination of Jorge Luis Borges. Do not operate heavy machinery for one hour after reading.

APPARITIONS: GHOSTS OF OLD EDO BY MIYUKI MIYABE

In old Edo, the past was never forgotten. It lived alongside the present in dark corners and in the shadows. In these tales, award-winning author Miyuki Miyabe explores the ghosts of early modern Japan and the spaces of the living world—workplaces, families, and the human soul—that they inhabit. Written with a journalistic eye and a fantasist's heart, *Apparitions* brings the restless dead, and those who encounter them, to life.

BATTLE ROYALE REMASTERED BY KOUSHUN TAKAMI

Koushun Takami's notorious high-octane thriller envisions a nightmare scenario: a class of junior high school students is taken to a deserted island where, as part of a ruthless authoritarian program, they are provided arms and forced to kill until only one survivor is left standing. Criticized as violent exploitation when first published in Japan—where it became a runaway best seller—*Battle Royale* is a *Lord of the Flies* for the 21st century, a potent allegory of what it means to be young and (barely) alive in a dog-eat-dog world. Now in a new, remastered translation by Nathan A. Collins.

WWW.HAIKASORU.COM